marked

"Marked," by Frederick Thomas. ISBN 978-0-9814554-0-2.

Published 2008 by Virtualbookworm.com Publishing Inc., P.O. Box 9949, College Station, TX 77842, US. ©2008, Frederick Thomas. All rights reserved. No part of this publication may be reproduced, stored in a retrieval system, or transmitted in any form or by any means, electronic, mechanical, recording or otherwise, without the prior written permission of Frederick Thomas.

Manufactured in the United States of America.

Saturday — December 4th

They stopped in at the 7-Eleven on their way home from the Target store tree lot. A nice six-foot fir was perched on top of their Honda Accord outside in the drizzling rain. It had taken them the better part of an hour to pick it out. Wes' wife had wanted the perfect tree.

The door chimed a warning to the guy behind the counter as they entered. Their wet tennis shoes squeaked on the linoleum. It's a Wonderful Life was playing on the little color TV up on a shelf next to the cigarettes. It was at the scene where George is up on the bridge considering killing himself.

The lanky clerk waved hello. Wes pointed at the guy's Santa hat and gave a thumbs-up to the holiday spirit. The clerk nodded in return.

Wes had grumbled when they were looking at trees but secretly he loved them. He'd never admit it to his wife but he liked the pine smell; it always made a house seem fresh and reinvigorated.

In the car, Wes had come up with the brilliant idea, or so he thought, of making 'Smores. So now they wandered up and down the aisles looking for marshmallows, chocolate and graham crackers.

The doorbell chimed again as another person

entered. Wes and Chiang-Mei could hear the tell-tale squeak of running shoes.

The clerk threw out his Christmas wave but it wasn't returned by the young man who was wearing a hooded jacket and shades. Shades in December? thought the clerk. Man, this can't be good, the clerk's mind responded.

Wes' wife Chiang-Mei shouted an, "Ah-Ha!" when she found the graham crackers. When she and Wes moved back toward the front to pay for their goods, they were surprised to see the clerk standing there behind the counter with his hands in the air.

They followed the clerk's line of vision back to its origin and saw a kid with a big gun.

The kid swung the gun in their direction and said, "Don't move motherfuckas. After this boy gives me the cash, y'all can be on your way. It's Christmas and I'm feeling generous so don't make me blast you."

Wes dropped the chocolate and marshmallows he'd gathered up. He didn't know if he believed the kid's sudden streak of kindness. He tried to talk to the diminutive gangster. He didn't want the youth to go through with the crime, much less get anyone hurt. Wes had done it before. Why should this be any different? he thought. After all, his intellect had always been his greatest ally and most devastating weapon.

"You don't want to do this, son," he had said in a relaxed even tone, maintaining eye contact. "Why don't you relax so we can talk about this."

"I'm cool as ice mutha-fucka," replied the hood wearing kid. "Yo', I got the gun. You the mutha-fucka need to keep yo' hands from shaking."

Wes took an involuntary glance down and saw that his hands were indeed shaking. He made fists to stop their slow shudders. He looked up at the smirking boy-man.

There were no other customers in the store. The cars and people passing by within inches outside seemed to have been in a whole other dimension. Perhaps, if someone had just glanced inside and then made a quick call on their cell-phone, but no. "Honey, don't. Just let it go," Wes' wife Chiang-Mei had pleaded.

"Yeah, listen to yo' bitch," the punk had sneered. His gun moved from Wes to Chiang-Mei to the lanky Santa behind the counter and back again. It was like a deadly game of eeny-meeny-miney-moe.

But Wes' ego just couldn't drop it. He knew he could win. He always did. Mind against mind, in any contest, Wes was the all-time champ.

Trying to peer behind the grey hood and sunglasses that masked the gangster's identity Wes said, "All I'm trying to say is that I've been where you're from and I know where you're going. And that's nowhere.

"That security camera has your face now. And a whole force of men and women out there paid by the city and county are going to get a copy. Then they're going to track you down and put you away if you don't get killed somewhere else along the way."

And truth be told, Wes hadn't lied just to establish a rapport with the kid. Once upon a time he had been in a gang. He had been one of the lucky ones. He had survived to tell the tale. If only he could get this kid to listen, but that last little bit had taken them all over the edge.

"What the fuck you sayin' nigga? You sayin' you better 'n me? With yo' fancy suit and 'I'm so smart' glasses. You think you runnin' shit?" the killer-in-training asked suddenly enraged. Perhaps the remnants of the marijuana he had smoked earlier in the day still fogged the youth's brain. In and out with the money quick had been the plan and yet...

"No, that's not..." Wes protested, but he was cut off.

"Nigga, you done forgot where you from. I think you need a little refresher. I'm runnin' shit here." And with that, the young gun pivoted the pistol in Chiang-mei's direction and fired.

The shots were deafening and then time seemed to standstill. It was like that movie the Matrix or something. Wes could somehow see the bullets as they emerged from the gun and slowly ran along their trajectory toward the intended victim.

Wes was about five feet from where Chiang-Mei was. He jumped into action and easily got his body in between hers and the bullets.

The pain was extreme.

From his vantage point on the floor, he could only see the gangster's white shoes as they bolted from the store. He looked up at Chiang-Mei. He tried to reach up and touch her face one last time but his arm wouldn't obey him. He could hear Chiang-Mei saying, "I love you" over and over again as he fell into darkness.

A loud outburst brought Wes out of his dream. "He's been restricted from any and all clearance. He single-handedly shut-down a sensitive military operation. He does not and I repeat, does not, have the clearance for this!"

"Lower your voice, Director. Don't forget who you're talking to."

Wes' eyes followed the sounds of the voices back into the kitchen where they had originated. He recognized the Senator and her husband. And the tall, graying gentleman was FBI Director, Karl

Brooks. He didn't recognize the Asian woman standing next to him.

I guess I fell asleep waiting for them Wes thought. He rubbed his eyes and went back over the dream. It was the same every time. In the dream, he manages to save her but in real life he had frozen up.

The bullets, after ripping through Chiang-Mei, had blasted some of the milk cartons in the freezer behind her. The milk and blood had mingled on the tile floor like melted strawberry-vanilla ice cream. Funny, the strange details you remember from catastrophic events.

The young store clerk had not moved one inch during the robber and Wes' short, heated exchange. When the gangster had fired his gun, the store clerk had dived under the counter and popped back up with a sawed-off, double-barreled shotgun. He put two booming blasts into the kid, killing him and destroying a rack of Hostess treats in the process. If not for the clerk, Wes would've been dead, too.

If he'd only kept his mouth shut and let the kid rob the 7-Eleven. It was only money. Who would it have hurt? If only, if only... Wes hit himself in the forehead with the palm of his hand.

He glanced down at the campaign button on the coffee table. Senator Cole hadn't formally announced her candidacy but everyone knew she was going to run for president.

"I'm sorry for raising my voice, Senator, but let Agent Yamazaki and her special team, handle this. If the media gets wind that this guy's working on the case, there'll be a feeding frenzy. He and the media are in bed together. Who knows what he owes them for the favors they did him. We can't take any chances with a washed up egghead," the Director said.

Brooks was a by-the-book man all the way. Or at least that's what he told himself. He had probably been born with a crew-cut. After the marines and getting his degree in political science, it was only natural that he'd become a G-man.

"I'm sorry, too, Karl, but that egghead you're referring to is maybe the smartest and most honest man I've ever met. Not to mention that he's one of the few people I trust in this world. If he's not a part of this investigation, I'll go to the media myself."

The Director scowled and then said, "Okay, okay, Senator, but he's just a consultant. I want that, at least, clear right now. He's not to interfere with this investigation. One wrong move and he's out."

"I can live with that, Karl."

Wes wondered what could be so serious.

The agents had dragged him out of bed at midnight the night before. They had told him that Senator Cole needed to see him right away. It was a matter of life and death. They had even sent a marine jet to bring him here from the west coast. But once he had arrived, the Director had balked at his presence.

Wes hadn't been sleeping well these past few days. The nightmares had come back. He had felt so tired when he had flopped down in the armchair to wait for the Senator.

Wes looked down at the rumpled clothes he had hastily thrown on. They looked like he felt.

Yamazaki nodded to the Director signaling that the person they'd all been arguing over was in fact, awake. They crossed the hall into the living room with the Senator and her husband close behind.

"All right, Mr. Washington. The senator trusts you and wants you in so you'll be a part of this investigation. But I remember the hearings and the news Mr. Washington. A lot of good men had their lives and careers ruined because of you. And the jury is still out on whether you were right or not.

"Before we go upstairs, you need to swear that whatever you may see or learn, in the course of this investigation, will be kept classified. And that's 'classified' as in you'll be sentenced to fifty years hard labor if any of this gets out, 'classified'. Do you understand?"

"Yep, all clear here," Wes replied while stifling a yawn.

Wes' compulsion for helping others and doing his civic duty always clashed with his disdain for authority.

The Director studied Wes disapprovingly for a few seconds more and then they all proceeded up the stairs.

They passed an agent at the second floor landing and continued on down the hall. It smelled strangely antiseptic and underneath that a hint of something else.

At the end of the hall stood two more feds wearing military redesigned Tyvek biohazard suits. The door and wall behind them had been replaced with a thick plexiglas airlock. Next to the feds on a long table were extra respirator masks.

Yamazaki passed them out. "Here, put this on," she said, as she handed one to Wes. "Actually, we're ninety-nine percent sure that she isn't contagious. And we don't think she's susceptible to outside bacteriological or viral contaminants either, but we're erring on the side of caution."

"*She's* not contagious?" Wes thought to himself. Then it was worse than he had imagined. He thought the senator's daughter Alex, had been away at school. Wes steeled himself for what he might see and entered the airlock.

Cool cleansing air whipped around them and was sucked back out by the ventilator. Wes could imagine someone sitting at a computer on the other side of that door signaling the all clear before the other door would be allowed to open. He had gone through the procedure enough to last a lifetime.

A moment later the door opened and they entered the room. Once it had been a large bedroom for a college girl. Now, where the dresser used to be, stood a ventilator. Where her bookshelf used to be was now an I.V. stand and a vitals monitor.

Inside the plastic covered medical bed rested a frail looking young woman. Wes had to stifle a gasp.

Wes moved closer to the bed. He could see the dark circles under her closed eyes and the swellings on her arms, neck and shoulders. Her face was ashy. Tubes and wires seemed to go everywhere. He whispered her name, "Alex..."

At the sound of his voice, her eyes fluttered open. Even though her body had begun to waste away, Wes was glad to see that the spark hadn't left her eyes. They were as bright as ever. She even tried to smile as she said, "Uncle Wes...."

"Don't talk, baby. Save your strength. I just wanted a look at those pretty little eyes of yours."

"Are you going to help me, Uncle Wes?" Alex asked, her voice barely a whisper.

Behind him Wes could hear the Senator stifle a sob as he answered, "Yeah, darling, me and these people. We're gonna try. We're gonna try *real* hard.

After spending a few more moments with Alex, they moved down the hall to the senator's home office. Her husband Greg stayed behind with Alex.

Wes pored over files of data as he sat at the senator's desk. After his visit with Alex, Wes had asked to see the files on her illness immediately.

Agent Yamazaki leaned against the door watching him. He didn't seem as impressive or dangerous as everyone seemed to believe. They were about the same age, but she never heard of him when she was at Berkeley.

She glanced at Director Brooks, standing next to the window on the other side of the room. He had his arms folded in silent protest. The Director had an almost palpable revulsion for Mr. Washington. Under any other circumstances, it would have been fun for her watching her usually stoic boss so hot under the collar.

The Senator sat in the chair across the desk from Wes. She related the recent events that had led to their current situation as she sipped coffee from a mug.

"She came to visit us for the Thanksgiving holiday weekend. When we picked her up at the airport last week on Wednesday, she seemed perfectly fine. As Thanksgiving Day wore on she started coughing a little. That night she was vomiting and had a pretty bad headache. Of course we thought it was the flu or a little underdone turkey.

"Our family doctor, Dr. Quan, was nice enough to come out and check on her. He agreed that it was probably the flu. He prescribed some medicine, plenty of fluid and rest. He left and a couple days later she was back to perfect health."

"And now...?"

"And now the doctors' say she's got bone cancer," Agent Yamazaki replied flatly from her spot by the door.

"She began getting some unusual bruising and swelling so we took her to the hospital for some tests," the Senator said.

From the documents the Senator and Director had provided to him, Wes picked out the film of the cancer biopsy. He held it up to the light and examined it closely. "There's something strange here..."

Yamazaki caught the Director's eye. The Director looked back with eyebrows raised.

"You can see where it isn't just the bone rapidly growing, the surrounding muscle is actually turning into bone. This isn't bone cancer; this is FOP, isn't it?" Wes asked looking at them all with naked surprise.

The Director sighed and loosened his tie. He pulled back the curtain a bit and peeked through at the coming dawn. He wondered how many more dawns he would live to see. But he was getting a little ahead of himself.

"What I said about you hurting our operation is true, Wes, but what the Senator said about you is true, too. You're one helluva smart guy.

"Yumiko, that is, Agent Yamazaki, has got advanced degrees in immunology and biochemistry from U.C. Berkeley. She's a certified forensic scientist, too. It took her two days to figure out what you just did in two hours."

Wes rubbed his tired eyes. "Thanks for the compliment but let's stop playing around, Karl. You could've told me about the FOP and saved us those two hours. If that was a test, I think I've passed it."

Outside in the hall muted footfalls and shuffling could be heard. The agents were changing shifts.

"The doctors had it all wrong. They misdiagnosed what was going on but we can't really blame them. This genetic disease is so rare that almost no one ever comes across it. I think we had to see for ourselves if we were wasting our time having you on the team," Yumiko volunteered.

"Okay, so why am I here? What do you expect me to do?" Wes asked.

"Senator Cole said that you saved the day in more ways than one during that whole Super Soldier debacle. You were even able to reverse some of the damage."

"That's true but I worked on those projects for a long time. I was intimately familiar with the build up so reverse engineering the process wasn't all that difficult.

"Besides, I'm no doctor or investigator. You've got teams of them running around," Wes said hopelessly.

"But that's just the point. We need someone who can think outside the box, someone with a fresh set of eyes. Take me for example. I couldn't see what was really going on because I had an expectation about what it was I was going to find. You didn't," Yumiko said.

Wes sighed heavily. "I guess you've got a point and I do want to help. I just... I just don't want to let anyone down."

Patting Wes' hand the Senator said, "I know you've had it hard these past few years, Wes. And I know it's especially hard on you this time of year. If you want to bow out, I'll understand and I won't think any less of you. But like I told Karl and now, I'm telling you, if there's anyone that can help my daughter, it's you. I know you can."

Wes held the Senator's eyes with his own but she didn't drop her gaze. Wes had known Alex since she was a little girl. She would've probably baby-sat for him if he and Chiang-Mei had had a child. Finally Wes broke eye contact and said, "All right, I'm in. Where do we go from here?"

"To the lab. Also, we've got most of the files you worked on with the Super Soldier Program thanks to Senator Cole and we're going to need you to fill in any of the blanks that are missing," Yumiko said. "But first maybe you'd like to catch a quick nap and then freshen up. We'll drop you at your hotel. We've already made arrangements."

———————

It was a lovely, brisk winter morning as the two girls played in the park. Their mother stood a few feet away watching them with a proud smile on her face.

The girls must have posed quite a pretty picture to see because besides the mother and the two highly paid security agents standing against the tree over there, there was another person watching as well. One of the bodyguards glanced in his direction and sized him up. She dismissed him as, a minimal to, no threat.

This person, watching the girls from the street side of the park, was a tall, slender black man wearing round-rimmed glasses. He was nibbling on a blueberry scone he had bought from the Starbucks around the corner. But this man wasn't just a casual observer of the girls' antics. He knew a lot about them actually.

For example, he knew it was the girls' birthday today. Tisha and Tiana were now eight years old. Late this afternoon, they were going to have a surprise birthday party with all their little friends. That's why they were at the park now, so the party could be set up without the girls being any the wiser. And also, this afternoon, unfortunately, they were going to be infected with a very baaaad disease.

How did he know this? He knew because he was going to infect them. He didn't want to of course, but the genie was out of the bottle now and it was time to make a wish.

One of the girls was wearing yellow mittens and a matching scarf. He guessed she was Tisha. She ran to the ladder of the yellow, corkscrew slide and quickly ascended. Tiana was right on her heels in a pink outfit that matched her sister's.

Once they were both at the top, Tisha sat and then Tiana straddled her from behind. Then as a unit, they slid down and around to the bottom, squealing in delight. After they hit the sandy bottom, Tiana jumped up and yelled, "That was great, let's do that again!" And they were off.

Watching the girls brought on a wave of nostalgia. He took another bite of his scone and tried to remember where that feeling was coming from.

He was an only child so it wasn't fond memories of playing with a sibling. A cousin perhaps? Or maybe a best friend? He wracked his brain as he watched the girls play. That feeling of nostalgia nagged at him but the memory wouldn't come. He dropped it. It would eventually come to him. It always did.

The second security agent ran her eyes over the scone man and dismissed him as well, at first. But then she looked at the man again a little harder. He's kind of staring off into space and he's not wearing gloves or a scarf in this cold, she thought. She whispered her intent to check up on the stranger to her partner and began walking in his direction.

I guess I've been watching a little too long, the man thought as he took another bite of the soft scone. The fake driver's license in his pocket read 'Harold Smith'. He had used so many aliases these past few years that his own name had begun to gently fade from his memory. He casually pulled a cell phone from his inner blazer pocket and spoke just loud enough for the approaching security agent to hear.

"Hello? What?! You can't meet me for breakfast... uh-huh... but I've been waiting here for twenty... uh-huh..."

The bodyguard had slowed her approach. Harold Smith continued into the phone, "So, how about dinner, then? Uh-huh... around eight... Me? I'll probably do some shopping before I head downtown... o.k. .... uh-huh... see you then."

He flipped the phone down and put it back in his pocket. The bodyguard had stopped about five yards from him, but she was still looking at him—hard. He knew if he checked to see if his act had worked, he would blow it, so he slowly turned and strolled away tossing the unfinished scone into a trash bin as he went.

The security agent's gaze followed him as he disappeared behind some trees lining the sidewalk. Probably a goddamn pedophile or something, the agent thought to herself. Those people were the worst kind of scum. They should all be killed.

She turned to her partner and shook her head slightly. Her partner shrugged in response. The guard watched the girls for a moment, scanned the street again and then made her way back to her partner.

Once clear of suspicion and danger, Harold tried to hail a passing cab. The cab driver saw him and even though his cab was empty, he kept right on going. Two more cabs passed Harold in the space of ten minutes but still wouldn't pick him up. Harold laughed. Here he had the keys to Pandora's Box but couldn't catch a cab. Finally, a black cab driver saw him and stopped. He climbed inside after it had pulled to the curb.

"Colonial Inn on Hudson, please."

"Yes, sir," the cabbie replied as he eased the taxi back into traffic.

Harold watched the skyline for a moment and then it slammed into him like a freight train. The memory. It wasn't his own childhood that had given him that nostalgic feeling. It was the memory of his own daughter playing and frolicking so sweet and innocent on a similar winter day.

"How could I have forgotten that?" Harold asked himself angrily.

"Whazzat, boss?" the cabbie asked.

"Sorry, nothing. Just talking to myself."

"Gotcha," the cabbie said before returning to his driving.

A tear threatened to burst forth as the memory danced in Harold's mind but he held it back. No, the time for tears is over, he thought. Now is the time for action.

Late that morning Wes was awakened by a knock at his downtown hotel door. He crawled out of the lumpy queen sized bed, threw on the hotel provided robe and let Yumiko in. She entered carrying a couple of coffees for them. The logo on the cup read: Ebenezer's Coffee House.

After a sip or two and a compliment about the coffee's taste, Wes slipped into the shower.

Yumiko strolled around the room as Wes showered. They were on the fourth floor and as she passed the window, Yumiko could see the

Washington monument off in the distance.

"We're going to stop by the lab and then later on in the afternoon I'd like to get your opinion on something," Yumiko called out when she heard the water stop.

"Okay, sounds like a plan."

Now that Wes was fresh, clothed and completely awake they took the elevator down to the garage and jumped into Yumiko's FBI sedan. She paused to put on her shades and took off.

"So how'd you wind up in the FBI, Agent Yamazaki?" Wes asked as he watched the morning traffic whip by.

"Yumiko's fine, and my father was in the bureau," she replied.

"Aaaahh...," Wes answered after a moment of reflection.

"What's 'aaaaahh' supposed to mean?" Yumiko asked looking at Wes through her sunglasses with a doubtful smirk on her face.

"Sorry," Wes shrugged in apology. "I didn't mean anything by it one way or another. Haven't been sleeping so too much thinking, I guess."

"No, please. We've got about twenty minutes. Let 'er rip," she said, half-mockingly as she merged onto the 395 highway.

Wes hesitated. "But you won't like it. I mean even though we probably won't become best buddies while I'm around, I'd rather not get off on the wrong foot from the jump, either."

Yumiko laughed. "You're going to say that my father was obsessed with his work, ignored me and so I got into the force to gain his love and approval, right? We have psyche profiles before we join and every six months thereafter. I know what my issues are.

"And don't worry about pissing me off. Better men than you have tried and failed," she added.

"Hey, that's pretty good. I'm glad you're comfortable with your being and so self-aware. It's going to help you down the road but that's not what I was going to say."

"Okay, big brain, now you got me curious. Tell me, I promise I won't shoot you or at least if I do it'll just be a flesh wound."

Wes glanced at her but she wasn't smiling. He couldn't tell if she was joking.

Wes felt he really shouldn't say anything at all but something about Yumiko piqued his interest.

"Okay," Wes said shrugging. "But remember you asked for it."

Wes' eyes grew distant and his voice sounded far away as he said, "You live alone on the outskirts of the art district. You like being near people but not a part of them. Playing with your cat, whose name is Mozart or Schubert, is how you wind down after a hard day at work. Watching foreign, preferably romantic, movies till three in the morning, while sitting on your couch eating chocolate ice cream in your sweats is how you spend most nights. On Saturdays, you and a girlfriend go shopping and do lunch in the city."

Yumiko looked at Wes, whose eyes had grown from distant to cold, pitch black as he continued. "Your obsession with work is a cover for your issues with intimacy, not approval. Your father didn't rob you of his love. He's robbed you of your ability *to* love."

Her mouth opened as if to say something and then snapped shut. In a rare moment Yumiko found her witty, sarcastic banter had escaped her.

Wes shook himself and his eyes cleared. They

were once more brown, bright and beautiful.

Yumiko opened her mouth again and this time the words came, "My cat's name *is* Schubert. How could you possibly know that? Did the Director or someone put you up to this? Are you playing a fucking joke on me?"

Wes raised his palms in defense. "No joke and I told you, you wouldn't like it."

Yumiko nodded. She was impressed and a little scared. "Damn, you sound like Hannibal Lechter or something. I can see what the Senator meant but really, how do you do that? Don't tell me you're a psychic?"

"No, I'm not a psychic. Part of it is just being observant and part of it is a kind of formula. It's pretty easy, really," Wes responded.

"How so?"

He took his glasses off and wiped the lenses with a finger as he thought about her question. He put his glasses back on and said, "People all think that they're very much different, but you can only have so many human characteristics and so many different environments."

"And what's that supposed to mean, braniac?"

Wes was glad to see that she could joke about it. Most people didn't recover so quickly. She was tough. "Well, you know the Zodiac right?"

"Yep, I'm a Gemini."

"Good, and I'm a Capricorn. There are twelve different character types in the Zodiac. How about the Chinese Zodiac?"

"Sorry, it slips my mind."

"Well, if you were born in 1975 like I was, then you'd be a rabbit. And this year, is the year of the Tiger. But again, notice, there's twelve."

"Okay, I'm with you so far," Yumiko said.

"But a lot of those character traits overlap. But I'll come back to that in a second. Next is the Japanese. Do you know what they base their character traits on?"

"Duh," Yumiko said pointing to herself, "Japanese woman here."

Wes laughed and said, "Sorry, but some third or fourth generation Japanese-Americans don't know."

"Well, I do and it's blood type."

"Right, A, B, A/B and O. But again let's dismiss some of the overlap and just say there are three. Now going back to the Zodiac's again. If we were to compare tiger characteristics with the rabbit's and Capricorns with Geminis, we'd see some similarities. I've looked at them and whittled down all the overlapping traits. How many Zodiac signs do you think I was left with?"

"Three?"

"Bingo and if we look at Christian religious mythology, we have the Holy Trinity. Again..."

"Three?"

"Now you're catching on. Do you play chess?"

"Yes, of course. It was practically a requirement in my household."

"Yeah, mine, too. Anyway, when you play, the possibility of moves seems almost endless, doesn't it? But now with chess playing supercomputers, we see that after the first few moves into the game, the computer can extrapolate and predict all of those remaining moves. Doesn't make the game very much fun, though."

"No, it doesn't," Yumiko agreed.

"But how does the computer do that? Well, you don't have an infinite number of pieces, you've got nine; each with a max of four moves. You've got one board with sixty-four squares on it, again, not unlimited. If our brains were like the computers, we could figure it out, too, but then who'd ever want to play chess, much less any game."

"Yeah, I see your point but how'd you figure me out?" she asked not seeing the connection.

"A person's type of character is the size of the board. The chess pieces are the character traits from the Zodiac signs; honor, loyalty, cleverness, etc. And the human being itself is the game being played. So, drum roll please?"

Yumiko tapped out a drum roll on the steering wheel.

"So, a human being is just a template. When you add the features and characteristics, it seems like each person is different in unlimited ways but really each person is very similar. And given a particular stimulus, will often react in a predictably similar way."

Yumiko nodded. It did make sense in a very strange way. "Impressive theory. I think you need to get out more, but impressive theory. Now how did it work on me?"

"Okay, let's start with 'you live alone on the outskirts of the art district'. You're not wearing a wedding ring and in the time I've been around you, you haven't mentioned a significant other. Women will always inform another single person that they're attached within hours, if not minutes of meeting them."

Yumiko raised her eyebrows and glanced at Wes.

"Now you can imagine all the reasons why that would be important in society, but the point here is that a woman will think that she's the only *one* who does that but all women do. So, when you didn't, that tells me that you live 'alone'."

Yumiko said, "Okay, keep going."

"Brooks said you went to Berkeley. He said it offhand and casually. Most people would probably have missed it, but my brain files those tidbits of info away for later.

"Now, you didn't go there just for academics. You went for the culture, too. Also, you said your dad was FBI, an authority type figure. He married someone more on the creative side for balance. So, you live in the art district.

"You like people but because you're a science buff and FBI, you come off really authoritative. You can't be around normal people for very long. They look at you like you're a narc when you go to parties, don't they?"

"Yeah, I'm ice water on any hot party," Yumiko had to admit.

"Don't worry, I know how you feel. My friends all say I have cop's eyes. When people meet me for the first time, they always think I'm a cop or a priest. I swear I can't ask a person the simplest of questions without their response encapsulating their entire life story."

Yumiko laughed and nodded. She could relate.

"Okay, the cat hair on your clothes tells me...?"

Yumiko winced at her gullibility. "I have a cat. Man, I should've guessed that one. But how did you know his name is Schubert?"

"Well, I could go into specifics, but sometimes the easiest way to think of it is in terms of comparison. If you've met someone who's a certain way and meet another person who's similar, then they probably are. It's like when they say everyone has a double somewhere. They're usually talking about appearances but it works for other character traits as well," Wes said.

"Which means?"

"I knew a girl just like you back in college and she had two cats, one named Mozart and the other named Schubert."

Yumiko laughed and shook her head. "It all seems a little too simple, but you say it usually works, huh?"

"Almost all the time. So you see, it's nothing really special. You could do it. The difference is that my mind just kind of does it automatically. Life's like a puzzle to me, I guess. I've always been fascinated at the inner workings of human nature. Subconsciously, I pick up a piece of a person here and another there and before long, I pretty much know who I'm dealing with."

"But doesn't that take the romance and mystery out of life, if at the end of the day we're all just variations on a theme?"

"Well, remember, I warned you first. I don't just spring this info on people. I don't do it too often, but actually, I think it's the opposite. People allow themselves to be caught up in the same old patterns and ideas because society demands it. By showing people themselves, it gets them out of a rut and they can really enjoy themselves. They can break out of the routines and do some amazing things."

"Are you saying I could do something amazing?" Yumiko teased.

"Yeah, maybe. Why not?" Wes shrugged and stared out of the window at the passing cars and morning sun.

Smart guy, Yumiko thought.

As they drove in silence to FBI Counter-bioterrorism Annex B Yumiko took the opportunity to ponder what Wes had said about her father. He was right in a way. Yumiko's father had been the first FBI field agent of Japanese descent. Yumiko's grandfather had been a boy in the internment camps. When he'd gotten out, he always went on about the injustice he and his family had suffered. Yumiko's father grew up and took that message to heart. He became part of the justice system, so that kind of injustice would never happen to his family again. But looking back, she could see how justice had become an obsession for her father. And in the end, that's all he had.

The regional office and lab was a refurbished old four-story hospital on 4th Street. FBI headquarters in the J. Edgar Hoover building was nearby on Pennsylvania street.

Of course, Annex B was state of the art. It had the latest DNA analysis equipment with a database of thousands of samples. After 9/11, whatever the feds wanted, they apparently got.

Their forensic section was light years ahead of any privately owned corporation Wes saw in passing some of the rooms as they headed on up to the third floor.

In administration at the back of the third floor Wes was issued a security badge and codes. He'd be able to gain access to most areas of the building and unclassified computer systems. Yumiko pointed out a small office including a computer station that had been specifically set aside for Wes. There was a desktop, laptop and Blackberry type PDA sitting on the cubicle's desk. Wes picked up the laptop and dropped the PDA into his tan sport-coat's pocket. Yumiko then led Wes downstairs to a conference room for the morning's briefing.

Once she was set and the last investigators and scientists had trickled in, Yumiko brought up a three-dimensional rotating illustration of the disease on the wall-screen.

Wes had taken a seat toward the back and flipped on the laptop. Through the wi-fied computer, Wes followed along on his own screen as Yumiko related the facts on hers. A few of the others in the room did the same.

"Although misdiagnosed as bone cancer, we've confirmed that Patient A is in fact suffering from FOP; fibrodysplasia ossificans progressiva."

With a few keystrokes Yumiko magnified the defective gene a million times.

"Usually, however, FOP is apparent at birth, by toes that are very short and point outward laterally. Symptoms can begin anytime during the first 25 years of life. The first signs are typically swellings on the arm, neck or shoulders accompanied by severe pain."

Yumiko switched the image to that of a nude person, whose face was obscured, who was exhibiting the disease and continued, "Mobility becomes progressively worse. Patients cannot raise their arms above their heads. Lung muscles are converted to bone which makes breathing more difficult. Removal of the bone simply accelerates the process."

The problem, Wes thought, as the image of the disease danced on his screen, was what was the cure? Because the disease contained the person's own DNA as the master template it would be difficult to destroy without harming the host's own genetic integrity.

The experiments that were done when Wes was involved in the Super Soldier program were designed more as upgrades, if you could call them that. They had dabbled with making a soldier's skin and bones tougher like an exoskeleton but those changes had been more in line with gene therapy. It had been far easier to restore those soldiers back to their former selves than this would be.

Splitting the screen in two, Yumiko displayed Patient A's treatment file which Wes knew was actually Alexandra's file. Wes saw that when the hospital had tried chemotherapy to suppress the growth, it had little to no effect.

"Life expectancy?" asked one of the scientists.

"Life expectancy is normally not dramatically reduced. FOP comes and goes throughout a person's life. Sometimes there are flare-ups and sometimes not."

"I understand that someone important has been infected but the gene responsible for FOP has been identified as ACVR1. That gene is responsible for a protein regulating bone protein. Universities around the world are researching this disease. This is a natural disease. What are we looking to accomplish here?" asked another scientist from the back of the room.

"The main problem in Patient A's case is that she manifested the disease so late in life. This is highly disturbing. Also, the manifestation is not running its normal course and has become life threatening."

There were murmurs and grumbles around the room.

Wes asked, "In what way?"

"FOP affects the neck, spine, chest, shoulders, elbows, wrists, hips, knees, ankles, jaw, and many similar areas. The progression follows a characteristic pattern. Usually extra bone forms in the upper areas like the shoulders before developing in the hips and knees. The muscles of the tongue, eyes, diaphragm, face and heart are characteristically spared.

"However," Yumiko said as she switched the

picture to a close up of some heart muscle cells, "it appears in Patient A's case that the heart is being affected."

The obvious signs of ossification could be seen in the picture. There were gasps from those in the room who knew who Patient A really was. Muted conversations circled around the room as Yumiko went on.

"At this rate of progress, we believe Patient A has about one week to live."

The noise level in the room jumped as the conversations morphed into heated discussions going back and forth.

Wes clicked on his screen to bring up the file on the current theory for a cure. Their answer so far had been to create an anti-cancer drug similar to Gleevec that would enter Alex's system and block the receptors from attack. But every computer simulated trial so far had ended in either an unstable drug or one ineffective against the disease. There was something missing.

But something else was missing too. Something Yumiko had *not* said in her presentation. Wes was used to the double-speak though. He had said some of it himself often enough when he was a government research rat. He gave up and imagined the notes to a piano piece he'd recently been learning to play to distract himself and then, bam, it came to him.

"You mentioned that it was 'highly disturbing' to you that Patient A had manifested the disease at such a late age. Why is that seemingly more disturbing than this person's impending death?" Wes asked.

Yumiko nodded and thought, Damn, he *is* quick. She said, "I was coming to that. If there are still some of you who aren't moved by the urgency of this young person's plight, be moved by this. We think that this disease is not in fact occurring naturally in this woman. We believe it is a new biological weapon; a possible terrorist attack. Domestic or otherwise."

The room practically exploded into a cacophony of questions. Why weren't we told this sooner? Does the President know? Can I warn my family? Who are the culprits?

They had it all; the best resources in the world but it would still take time. And time was the one thing that they didn't have. Yumiko advised them that much of what they were going on was speculation and anyone who spread unfounded rumors would be remiss in their duties as Department of Justice representatives. Also, they'd be subject to disciplinary action. Everyone calmed down at that point and Yumiko was able to finish the last of her report on Patient A.

At the presentation's conclusion Wes asked, "Excuse me, Agent Yamazaki?"

"I'm sorry, I don't think I've introduced our new consultant. This is Dr. Wes Washington," Yumiko said gesturing in his direction.

Wes nodded a general greeting and asked, "Have the other cases been identified?"

"What other cases, Wes?" Yumiko asked.

"Well, I was thinking about it and I'm sure you have, too. This is a genetically engineered weapon. It was specifically designed for Patient A; someone of value in a political sense," Wes continued, the greased wheels in his head were spinning.

"Ah, yes, I see where you're going. Yes, people in sensitive positions or areas within the government with proper clearance have all been notified but there are no other cases."

"No, I don't think you do see. What makes you think that Patient A was the first? Perhaps the killer tested out this weapon on some nobody as a trial just to see if it would work. Have the morgues been searched?"

Heads around the room were nodding at Wes' proposition.

"You're assuming these criminals are a domestic threat but that hasn't been established definitively, Mr. Washington," Yumiko said slightly embarrassed at being caught off-guard.

"You said what you knew was speculation Agent Yamazaki so a domestic threat is a possibility, isn't it?" Wes shot back.

"Yes... and in fact, we're going to interview a possible domestic terrorist later on today. I want you to tag along so I can get your assessment of him. But without any evidence we don't want to alarm anyone unnecessarily. In any event you make a good point."

Yumiko paused for a moment to regain her composure and then said, "Agent Gonzalez, put some analysts on searching hospitals, morgues and funeral homes. Put them on notice to notify us of any deaths caused by leukemia, cardiac, lung or oncological disease, etc., within the past year."

"Yes, ma'am", the muscular, green-eyed agent replied as he stood and left the room.

"If we can obtain the prototype for this biological weapon, we can track the design and come up with a treatment more easily. Or at the least we can work on a vaccine for the future victims," Wes explained.

Yumiko shook her head and said, "Our profiler's best analysis so far is that this is a group whose next move is to hold America hostage when their weapon is perfected. They're a sub-splinter group of the now defunct Al-Qaeda. They believe in Al-Qaeda's philosophy but aren't as committed to the sacrifice. Ransom in the billions of dollars, is their immediate goal. And we're going to catch them. There aren't going to be any more victims."

"I'm sorry to burst your profiler's bubble but this is not about national or political terrorism. There's something else going on here. This is personal and it's not gonna stop until the killer says so," Wes replied.

"Well, I hope you're wrong," Yumiko said, turning off the wall-screen. "A group is much easier to nab than some nut-job with a personal vendetta. We don't want another Unabomber or Timothy McVeigh on our hands."

"You and me both," Wes said under his breath, but he knew better.

The meeting broke up then and after a quick bite at the cafeteria, Wes met Yumiko outside in the parking lot.

Agent Gonzalez whom Wes had seen earlier was sitting in a car parked next to Yumiko's. The raven-haired woman sitting next to him was his partner Suzette Abrams. They were waiting to accompany Yumiko as backup.

As Yumiko and Wes climbed into her vehicle, he said, "I wanted to say I'm sorry if it got a little heated in there."

Yumiko waved it off as she buckled up. "No problem. We've even come to blows in debriefing. We disagree on method but at the end of the day we know we're all on the same side. We do our job. We always get our man or woman as the case may be."

"So, where to?" Wes inquired as they left the lot and sped along.

Yumiko pulled onto the Capital Beltway and

said, "University of Maryland. We're meeting Dr. Greeley. He's a professor at their Center for Advanced Research in Biotechnology. He had been working on a project involving stem cell research and cloning under a government grant issued by the Department of Defense.

"Three years ago, when the DoD had decided to reduce funding for his project, he had written scathing letters to the members of the DoD and Senator Cole. Greeley had reluctantly apologized when the university put pressure on him. The file is on your PDA if you want to review the details."

"Do you seriously suspect Dr. Greeley?" Wes asked as he checked the side mirror to see the other agents following close behind.

"Well, there's always a chance but the guy just blew a fuse. Been in the lab too long. However, he may know something that he doesn't know he knows, so we're better playing it safe than sorry," Yumiko said.

"Back to your international terrorist theory?" Wes asked.

"If an enemy agent got next to him and bribed or blackmailed him. Yeah, could be," Yumiko declared.

Wes considered that in silence. He pulled out the PDA and started reading the file on Dr. Greeley.

"By the way," Yumiko said, "I forgot to ask. How did you know about FOP?"

"During the years when I was a fulltime researcher, one of the best ways to get ideas for our projects was to study genetic disease. Diseases and mutations produce some spectacular changes in organisms. We would try to emulate the way diseases functioned but in a controlled way to get the specific results we wanted. We were trying to... I mean... Anyway, that's how I came across FOP," Wes answered before turning back to Dr. Greeley's file.

Creative, Yumiko thought, but also disturbing.

A few minutes later they turned onto the campus grounds.

Yumiko and Wes climbed out of her sedan after they had parked near the science building. Gonzalez and Abrams parked next to Yumiko. As Yumiko and Wes started up the path they followed at a few paces behind.

The sounds of the agents polished shoes echoed as they strode along the science hall. It was a little empty for the Saturday before finals but Wes chalked it up to the students all studying at the library or the student union. They found Dr. Greeley's office and knocked.

"Post here, Suzette," Yumiko said to Agent Abrams. Abrams understood the order for what it really meant: make sure they weren't disturbed.

It was Agent Abrams' first assignment working with Yamazaki on such an important case even though she'd been with the bureau for four years. Her face showed no emotion but inside she was praying she'd do a good job and not screw anything up.

Dr. Greeley called out, "It's open. Come on in," and they entered. Greeley was seated in a beat-up leather chair at his desk and was laboring over some paperwork.

"Thanks for agreeing to meet with us, Dr. Greeley. I'm Agent Yumiko Yamazaki and this is Agent Matt Gonzalez," Yumiko said as she shook Greeley's hand. Agent Gonzalez didn't bother to acknowledge the professor, playing bad cop to Yumiko's good one. "And this is Professor Washington. You wouldn't happen to know each other would you? You run in the same circles."

Dr. Greeley squinted at Wes from behind his wide-framed glasses and scratched the back of his thinning head. The small, portly professor didn't look much like a domestic terrorist. His eyes betrayed knowledge, not malice, as he answered in a high, hushed voice, "No, I don't believe so. Although, the name does ring a bell. Perhaps I've read your published work somewhere?"

"It's doubtful. I mostly worked for the government and you know how they are about publishing," Wes replied.

Ed Greeley nodded in sympathy and understanding. The scientists did all of the work but got none of the glory.

A cell phone rang out a Brahms tone in Dr. Greeley's pocket. "Oh, sorry, I thought I had turned it off," he said with some embarrassment. Yumiko nodded for him to answer.

Dr. Greeley spoke into the phone and looked at Yumiko sheepishly.

Wes went back over in his mind what he'd read in the file while the professor conversed. Professor Greeley had been taken in for questioning by the FBI a few years ago in response to threatening e-mails that Senator Cole had been receiving. Funny, Wes thought, that the Senator had never mentioned it to him. He had thought they had become friends back then. She probably hadn't wanted to worry him with something he couldn't do anything about. But still...

The e-mails had used words like "obtuse" and "ignorant" in describing Senator Cole's lack of understanding about the scientific importance of Dr. Greeley's work. The e-mails were condescending but otherwise harmless, until they started mentioning "action being taken" and things being blown up.

Claiming that he had been stressed out due to

pressure at work and marital problems, Greeley wrote a formal apology to the Senator. The FBI dropped their investigation into Greeley but kept an open file on him.

"We appreciate your making time to speak with us on such short notice," Yumiko said as Greeley returned the phone to his pocket.

"Oh no, it's no trouble. After everyone was so kind to me during that... difficult episode in my life, I feel like I owe you over at the bureau. Anything I can do to help," Greeley said, nervously.

"We'd just like to ask you a few routine questions. Nothing related to that previous matter, by the way," Yumiko offered.

Agent Gonzalez was peering closely at one of the diplomas on the wall above and to the right of Dr. Greeley's head to make the doctor even more jumpy.

Gonzalez' theory was that people were prone to more slip-ups and mistakes in their story when they were nervous. Gonzalez also thought that everybody was guilty. His philosophy was, if someone rolled up on you and shot you, you did something to someone. Maybe you didn't know it at the time, but there was always a reason.

"Okay, please go ahead. And sit, sit," Greeley said and laced his fingers on his lap to keep them from shaking.

Yumiko and Wes took the two seats in front of the professor's desk. There was a chair in the corner, but Gonzalez ignored it and kept roving, pausing only for a moment or two now and again.

"Can you tell us your whereabouts in the days before, during and after this past Thanksgiving?" Yumiko asked in a business-like fashion.

The questions continued in that way for another hour or so. Yumiko was nothing if, not thorough. She enjoyed her work and did it well. She backtracked to try to catch Greeley in a lie, three or four times by Wes' count.

It turned out that Greeley was visiting his sister and her family down in Florida from November twentieth until the twenty-seventh. Of course he could have secretly driven back to do the deed. Or he might have an accomplice but his answers made it doubtful.

They were nearing the close of the interview when Yumiko's cell phone rang. She excused herself and stepped out into the hall. A moment later she came back in and said, "Well, thank you for your time, Professor Greeley. If we need more information, we'll let you know."

Yumiko left with the agents and Wes in tow as Greeley mumbled a half-hearted goodbye.

As they walked to their vehicles, Agent Gonzalez asked, "So, what's up, boss?"

"We got a hit on one of those hospital cases you had them start checking this morning Gonzalez; a real strong one. The Agent-in-charge wants us to follow up ASAP. Turns out the daughter of the head of a pharmaceutical company died a few months back from bone cancer. Also, the company head was involved in government projects back in the eighties and early nineties," Yumiko replied.

"Sounds like we caught a break," Abrams added.

"Yeah, they're going to exhume the body as soon as we get the court order," Yumiko said.

"What about the father?" Wes asked. "People usually freak out at the prospect of exhuming a family member. Won't he protest?"

Yumiko checked her watch. It was 3:30 p.m.

"Unfortunately, we caught a break there, too. Shortly after his daughter died, the father, the only living relative, killed himself," Yumiko said. "We're going back to the office. Let's go."

Wes could only shake his head in wonder as they got into the car.

———————

Bolting upright and awake, a scream slowly died in Harold's throat. He found himself drenched in sweat. For a moment, as he looked around, his eyes blinking in the dim light, he forgot where he was. As his bare chest grew cold under the hotel room's air-conditioning, he remembered.

Shaking himself, he yawned and sprang out of bed. He didn't bother glancing at his watch over on the nightstand. His internal clock was programmed to perfection. Before he had taken his nap a couple of hours ago, he had told himself to wake up at 11:30 a.m. So, he had no doubt that that was exactly what time it was, minus the few seconds he had taken to re-orient himself.

Taking naps throughout the twenty-four hour day as opposed to sleeping the whole night away kept him rested and alert. It also gave him an advantage over his would-be pursuers. When they were all asleep, he was working. And he was working hard.

He had read somewhere that Edison did the same thing when he was consumed by a project. Probably slept like that when he was working on the bulb. Only difference between Harold and Edison was that Harold was smarter. The triumphs of the greatest minds in the world would pale in comparison to what Harold was about to do.

Harold adjusted the air-conditioning and then went into the closet. He pulled out his suitcase and laid it on the double bed. He unlocked and opened it.

Inside the suitcase was a clown suit, big red floppy shoes and all. He had thought of multiple ways to enter Eric King's estate and get access to the girls. He had considered going in as a server, a security guard and even as a guest, but he felt the clown disguise gave him the maximum chance of success. His delivery system was airborne so he didn't have to get within inches, but he still had to be within a few feet.

He gave the rest of the contents of the case another once over and then closed it, satisfied that all was in order.

As a boy, he had been terrified of clowns. Funny how that is; you either love them or hate them. There's not that much wiggle room when it comes to clowns. But Harold's ultimate nightmare had long ago been realized and now fear's cold dark hands held no sway over him.

After a quick shower, he changed into dark gray sports slacks and a gray sweater. It was always more difficult for people to remember neutral colors. He considered wearing the fake glasses he had worn this morning. After all those years in the labs staring at microscopic organism, he was surprised that his vision was still 20-20. He figured the agent who took a good look at him in the morning might recognize the frames, so he decided against it.

Pulling his door shut with suitcase in hand, Harold made his way down to the lobby. In the elevator two days ago, he had acquired one of the hotel employee's card keys. Since then, he had changed the face and name to match his own.

He had become quite the criminal. After much practice he had become an accomplished pickpocket, burglar and master of disguise. He wondered what dear old mom would have thought of the career change and laughed bitterly.

From the bank of lobby elevator, he walked around the corner to the service elevators. When he was confident he was unobserved, he swiped the card across the security scanner and gained access to the sub-basement where the employee parking garage was housed.

When the doors opened, he stepped boldly out of the elevator. There was no way he could know whether or not someone would be in the garage short of bugging the place. Unfortunately he hadn't had time for that so his lie of being a new employee was at the ready instead.

No one was in the garage now, but he smelled a faint trace of cigarette smoke. Whoever owned that scent could return at any moment so Harold didn't dawdle.

Quickly, he made his way to the service bay. There was a wooden board with keys hanging from its hooks up against the bay's back wall. The board was used for checking out the various hotel vehicles. He scanned the numbers and then plucked one of the keys off of the board.

From there, he made his way to one of the three empty hotel service vans parked in the south corner under dim lighting. He jumped into the van and threw his suitcase into the back. He started it up and drove up to the automatic gate. When the gate opened, Harold drove out into the overcast day.

On the outskirts of Bethesda, Harold had stopped at a gas station. The first thing he had done was switch the van's license plates with ones he'd acquired from a junkyard days ago. Then, he had gone into the restroom and changed into his clown suit. In front of the polished metal plate that served as a mirror, he had carefully applied the clown makeup and adjusted his outlandish wig.

He had also taken the folded magnetic sign from the bottom of his suitcase and pasted it over the hotel's logo. The van now read: Quicksand Entertainment.

Now, as he pulled up to the retired general's estate and pressed the buzzer he had to hold in a laugh at the inside joke. Too bad he had no one to share it with. Ah, well.

The estate was about two acres. The hundred year old home was colonial style constructed from brick and wood. There was an extensive English garden, stone and brick walkways, a pool and a guest house.

An armed guard popped out of a booth behind the iron-wrought, electrified gate as Harold edged up closer to it and killed his engine.

As he waited for the security guard who had a clipboard in hand, to come through the side metal door, Harold could see many luxury cars already parked in the circular driveway. The party was well underway inside the sprawling compound. Faint sounds of music and children's screams of joy floated to him across the manicured lawn.

The security guard tapped on the driver's side window with a knuckle. "Hey, buddy, roll down your window," the guard said, speaking loudly and mouthing the words. Rolling down the window, Harold read the name William off of the gold-plated badge pinned to the guard's chest. The name didn't quite match up with the overweight body attached to it.

William offered a thin smile as he asked for Harold's name and purpose of visit.

Through his bright red clown smile and a fake,

heavily accented northeastern drawl, Harold said, "Smith, Harry Smith."

"Well, Mr. Smith," the guard said, looking at his clipboard and glancing at the side of the van, "We don't seem to have that name or Quicksand Entertainment on the list."

"Yeah, someone just called it in this morning. You might want to check again. This happens sometimes with these last minute gigs," Harold said, with the red smile never wavering. He thought that he might have been an actor in a past life.

The security guard looked at him with a skeptical eye as he said, "Well, I'll check again. We wouldn't want to disappoint the kids."

"Nope we sure wouldn't want to do that. No sirree," Harold said with a hint of mockery in his tone. William's eyes narrowed a bit and his right hand slid down toward his gun belt.

The adrenaline was pumping him up and old Harry had the pedal to the metal. He decided to throttle back a bit. Dropping the shit-eating grin instantly he said, "I have a couple of kids myself. I'm taking them to the game after this. I wouldn't be working on the weekend at all except one of my employees called in sick."

That seemed to do the trick. In one fell swoop, old Harry was a hard-working business owner trying to put food on the table for his all-American, apple pie eating, football loving family.

"You a Redskins fan?" William asked his hand easing away from the gun belt.

"Used to be, before all the free agents ruined the game."

"Ain't that the truth," William said. "They whine and cry like a bunch of babies but you don't see 'em offering to give back any of those million dollar signing bonuses. Okay, wait here a sec'. I'll be right back."

Harold breathed a sigh of relief as the guard popped back into his pillbox to check his computer. He'd find Harold Smith and Quicksand Entertainment on the list now. Harold had only hacked the computer late last night. If he had done it sooner, someone might've noticed and run a thorough check on his non-existent company. He'd go back in and erase the file this evening.

The gate, making a slight grinding noise, began to roll back on its metal wheels. William popped back out of his booth and approached Harold again. This guy's like a goddamn Jack-in-the-box Harold thought.

When he reached the driver's window, William said, "Looks like you were right, somebody must've called you in at the last minute. Sign here and go on up."

Harold signed an illegible scribble in the space William had indicated on the paper. Then, he started the van and pulled forward.

"Hey, enjoy the game with your kids," William said throwing Harold a brief grin.

'What kids?' is what Harold felt like saying but instead said, "Thanks, I will." And he flashed the guard a grin in return.

There was a guy in a server's uniform throwing some garbage out as Harold pulled around to the service entrance in the back. Harold waved a service comrade-in-arms hello, and parked between a ten year old Honda Civic and a catering van.

When the server had gone back inside, Harold climbed through the seats and into the back. He jostled the balloons he had bought from the party store back in Bethesda.

marked   41

He opened his suitcase and pulled up a corner of the inside. Hidden in the case's corner was a small lead compartment. Harold unlatched and opened the compartment. He took out a small leather herb sack. The sack attached easily to his costume belt by its drawstring.

From there, Harold grabbed a fistful of balloons, hopped out of the van and shut the doors. The stench of the garbage caused him to wrinkle his nose in disgust. Then, he bounded up the steps and entered the kitchen.

Smells of bread and tomato sauce wafted into Harold's nose as he glided through the stuffy and hot kitchen. He gave a balloon to one of the female servers as he went by. She giggled as the rest of the kitchen crew looked on laughing.

After he went through the double doors at the front of the kitchen, he followed the sounds of cavorting children.

Actually, he had memorized the blueprint of the home just in case he needed a quick exit. He knew where all the doors and windows were located but he allowed himself to wander and after a time, he found himself in a large living room.

The birthday girls were seated on a couch toward the back of the room. They were wearing the same dress, but in different colors; one yellow and the other pink. And they had matching bows in their hair, too. They were as cute as buttons and just about to open their presents when Harold had arrived. Perfect timing.

The universe was smiling on Harold. Harold believed in a higher power but not in the same way that Muslims, Christians or any other religious group believed in it. Harold felt that there was simply a natural order to the universe and that if you followed it, then most of your actions would turn out all right. Likewise, going against that natural law would seal your fate; quick.

One of the children by the living room entrance saw Harold and exclaimed, "It's a clown!" That little boy was rewarded with a nice, red balloon. Then, Harold did a roll into the middle of the room.

The retired general's wife smiled.

Never speaking, the clown danced and frolicked around the room pulling coins from children's ears and flowers from their parent's hair. Everyone watched transfixed as he pulled boiled eggs out of his mouth and stuffed sharp objects up his nose. The children shouted in amazement as he did back-flips and somersaults. He even gave a beautiful scarf from his sleeve to the security agent who had given him the once over this morning. She smiled briefly for the kids' sake and didn't register an ounce of recognition.

But, Harold was pushing his luck. It was time for the coup de grace. He back-flipped again and this time, landed on his knees in front of the twins. He slowly stood and raised his hands in a gesture of pause to silence the small crowd.

He unhooked the small leather bag from his belt and showed the room. Some of the younger children gasped in anticipation.

He raised his right hand, palm up and poured the contents of the bag onto it. A triangular pile of sparkling dust formed on his palm. He bent down so one of the smaller children could look at the dust carefully. The girl looked up at Harold with big, wide eyes. Harold's white painted face raised a questioning eyebrow in response. The little girl looked at the pile again and then whispered, "Fairy dust?"

Harold smiled broadly with approval. Then, with a spin and a flourish, the room was filled with beautiful, rainbow colored, sparkling fairy dust.

The kids shouted and danced as the fairy dust rained down around them. The parents gaped in wonder. Harold's eyes, however, never left the twins.

And then it happened; Tisha sneezed first, followed closely by Tiana. Harold wondered for a moment if they were born in that order. And then he wondered if they would die in that order, too. And then, he smiled.

Harold bowed for the audience as they clapped. He then turned on a heel and walked away. He was almost to the kitchen door when he heard, "Excuse me. Excuse me, sir?"

At first, assuming he was busted, Harold was going to pretend he hadn't heard and bolt out of the back door. But if it was nothing and he ran, he'd bring unnecessary suspicion down on himself before his mission was complete. He calculated the hundreds of different probabilities within the space of about a nanosecond. He estimated that there was more than a ninety percent chance that the person behind him was the girls' mother and turned around.

Damn I'm good, Harold thought as the ex-general's wife said, "Hi. I'm the twins' mother, Charlene King."

Harold shook her outstretched hand as one of the bodyguards looked on from a few paces away.

"I just wanted to say thanks and give you a little something," Mrs. King said and held out a folded bill.

Waving and shaking his hands, Harold indicated that he didn't want the money. Mrs. King said, "No, I insist. You did a wonderful job. What's your name by the way? And do you have a card? I'd like to recommend you to some of the other parents, if you don't mind."

Figuring she'd find it unusual for a working stiff to refuse a tip, Harold took the money. In response to her questions, which he had already anticipated, he made the 'shhhh' gesture with his finger and pointed at a picture of her husband on the wall.

"Oh, I see," Mrs. King said catching on. "My husband wants to keep it a secret."

His rainbow wig bounced up and down comically as Harold nodded.

"Okay, well, thanks again. And maybe we'll see you again next year, if the girls haven't gotten too big for clowns," Mrs. King said laughing.

He doubted he'd ever see Mrs. King in person again but nodded comically once more anyway.

Harold managed to get to his van unaccosted and drove back to the gate. William saw him coming and opened the gate in anticipation. Harold gave a brief thumbs up to William as he passed through and drove away from the compound.

Along the way back to the city, Harold stopped behind a Chinese restaurant and changed clothes in the van. He used some alcohol wet naps to remove the makeup. Then, he ditched the suitcase, sign, clown outfit and anything else he could think of that could tie him to the day's events in the restaurant's trash bin. Finally, he switched out the license plates and threw them down a nearby sewer drain.

He jumped back in the van and headed on. As he got into the city proper he took the van to a hand car wash. The young guys at the wash vacuumed and cleaned the van with zeal. They left plenty of fingerprints as well. Harold hoped the feds would go nuts trying to separate them all if the van was ever found. The wash guys earned themselves the same bill Mrs. King had given Harold.

Across the street and midway up the block from the hotel, Harold parked the van. He gave everything he may have touched another once over wipe and dropped the keys on the floor. He opened the door and locked it. He got out and shut it. He figured that when they discovered the van, they would think some idiot ran out for a bite to eat after washing it and locked themselves out. And then didn't report it to hide their embarrassment.

Whistling to himself, Harold strolled back to the hotel.

——— ——— ———

That night, as the ex-general unpacked, his wife said, "The girls really missed you today, Eric."

"Yeah, I know. I'm really sorry I missed it, hon. I thought I could get a flight back in time, but the meeting ran long and then the flight was delayed due to mechanical problems. It took them two hours to get another plane ready."

"So how did your meeting go?" Charlene asked as Eric hung up his suit.

"Well, the board decided to put off the merger with India Oil for now. They say the political climate isn't right," he replied.

"Oh, and thanks for getting them that clown. I thought they might be getting too old for that kind of stuff, but they seemed to really enjoy it," she said pulling down the covers on their bed.

Eric turned and looked at his wife questioningly, "What clown?"

——— ——— ———

Later that evening, about the same time that Harold was removing his name from the security guard's computer, Wes and Yumiko were down in the morgue.

They had gotten a federal judge (who hadn't been in the least pleased as he was on winter vacation) to sign their order to exhume Flora Wilhelm's body from a cemetery over in Rockville. The body had been flown back to the morgue by helicopter.

"There are signs of swellings on the arm, neck and shoulders," the medical examiner reported as Wes and Yumiko looked on.

"According to the records," Yumiko said, "She was initially admitted to the hospital with a broken right wrist after a fall, Eva." Yumiko's voice sounded gruff and husky through the mask she held to her face.

"That would be consistent with what I've found here although on a subsequent visit, the hand above the same wrist was amputated. It was believed to be overrun with a malignant form of cancer."

"We'll need a sample of the DNA, Dr. Maugh," Wes' muffled voice said through his mask.

"I had samples sent up as soon as the autopsy was started," she replied.

"How about COD, Eva?" asked Yumiko.

"The cause of death was a combination of pulmonary and cardiac failure. Her lungs and heart had started to petrify."

Wes and Yumiko locked eyes briefly.

"Okay, I think we've seen enough," Yumiko said. "Let's head back upstairs to a meeting room I had Matt set up for our use."

Wes followed Yumiko out to the main hallway. They discarded their masks in the biohazard trash and then took the stairs.

The moment he entered the room, Wes' cell phone rang. "Hello," Wes answered.

"Hi, Wes. Are you guys making any headway?" asked Senator Cole. The stress could be plainly heard in her voice.

Yumiko walked over to the two big whiteboards on the front wall of the room.

"Hi Janet," Wes said, "I'm sorry to say that so far the investigations haven't led anywhere, but we got a new lead this afternoon so..."

The Senator sighed heavily and then said, "I can't help but think somehow this is my fault and I feel so damn helpless. If there's anything you can do Wes."

"How's she doing?" Wes inquired.

"Not too well, I'm afraid," the Senator replied. "We've had to move her to a quarantined area at the University of Maryland hospital. They're keeping her comfortable and put her on a bunch of different anti-viral medications."

Funny how things work, Wes thought. They had just been at the university. Fate, destiny, call it whatever you want but somehow events were all tied together one way or another.

"That's good." Wes said. "They're giving her a variant of the AIDS cocktail. It can block the virus from attacking."

"Oh, hold on a sec, Wes."

Wes could hear voices in the background. When the Senator came back on the line, she said, "The doctor told me that Alex is awake and asking for me. I better go."

"No problem. She needs you. Tell her I said hang in there and I'm thinking of her," Wes said. "I'll call you the second I know anything."

Wes ended the call and turned to Yumiko.

"Tough kid, huh?" Yumiko asked.

"Yeah, she's a fighter. I think we're gonna beat this," Wes declared.

Taking a magnet from the corner of the board on the left, Yumiko put up a photo of Flora. In Gonzalez' room preparations he had left them a photo file along with other statistical information.

Next to Flora's photo Yumiko put up the photo of Alexandra Cole. Underneath their photos she arranged the photos of their parents. She wrote 'military' and 'science' under the photos.

"Well, we've got some obvious parallels going on here. Although the results aren't back, yet, this can't be a coincidence," Wes said nodding to himself.

"Both victims female, one or both of the parents involved in some of kind of scientific military issue," Yumiko agreed.

To make sure no one else was within earshot, Yumiko glanced around. She then said conspiratorially, "Speaking of the military, I heard about the hearings where you testified in front of Cole and the other intelligence committee members. Most of it was closed testimony because of the classified nature of the things you were working on. Some of my buddies over in the CIA said the Super Soldier experiments were off the charts, but what was it really?"

"I could tell you, but then..." Wes shrugged and smiled.

Yumiko laughed and said, "Yeah, right. You and what army?"

"Seriously though, it's something I can barely talk about because it borders on the horrific. You may have noticed I avoided your question earlier this afternoon. But if it helps..." Wes said sitting on a table. "I saw things that would make your hair stand on end. Permanently.

"At first, the only thing I was involved in was trying to regenerate tissue. The applications besides the military were enormous. Can you imagine the numbers of people around the world that this procedure could help? Going into a hospital to have surgery and have your own tissue regenerate itself?"

Yumiko nodded that she could imagine it.

"Well, we made some limited progress in that area with a mixture of cloning and nanobyte technology. A massive injury that would normally take weeks to heal was reduced to days. The military wanted it down to hours and minutes but we could never break the cell death barrier. You know a cell can only take so much poking and prodding before it says to hell with it and commits suicide so to speak."

Yumiko smiled and Wes continued, "So, anyway they see that although they didn't get what they wanted, the boy genius, Wes Washington, is too clever to be let go. He's sent to work on the *real* projects that they were having the most problems with. You ever read or see, The Island of Dr. Moreau?"

"Of course," Yumiko said, "but you don't mean?"

Wes stared off at nothing as he said, "Yeah, just picture it in reverse. Moreau was trying to make animals into humans. What we did to those poor prisoner soldiers... Did you know cats really can't see in total darkness? They just enhance what light there is. So they increased the size of a lion's eyes and implanted them in this unlucky guy's head."

Yumiko sucked in her breath.

"Another guy they gave gills and webbing to, for obvious reasons. Talk about your Navy Seal. But their hope of a part land, part sea creature never materialized. The moment this guy was out of the tank for more than a few seconds, he would start to suffocate because his lungs no longer functioned.

Yumiko shook her head in disgust.

"But the freakiest thing I ever saw was the guy whose bones were on the *outside* of his body. That's when we were working with FOP. They got obsessed with creating a soldier who had a built-in, exoskeleton type armor and..."

Yumiko cut Wes off. "Okay, okay! I don't think I want to know any more. I thought the germs and diseases I deal with everyday were bad."

Wes shivered. "Sorry about that, got a little carried away. The ironic part about it all was that none of it would've even been possible without the cell regeneration Super Soldier Serum or 'Triple S' as they nicknamed it. Most of their ultimate warrior ideas were just stuff on a drawing board until then. After Triple S, they could do all kinds of experiments with almost unlimited time on the operating table because the brain and heart were stable for hours on end.

"That's why I blew the whistle and went to Senator Cole's military intelligence committee. Somebody had to expose what they were doing in that laboratory and stop it. At least for awhile, anyway," Wes finished.

"What do you mean for awhile?" Yumiko asked.

"You don't think they ever really stopped, do you?" Wes asked cocking his head to one side as he turned and looked at Yumiko.

Yumiko's naiveté was a little disturbing. Perhaps growing up in a household where your father was a federal agent would do that to you. Make you all trusting of the government; at least until their hammer came down on you, too.

"Well, with all the media attention..." Yumiko proposed.

"True but people forget. And honestly, they never really wanted to know in the first place..." said Wes whose voice had stopped suddenly.

Misinterpreting Wes' sudden silence, Yumiko said, "Are you all right. If you don't want to talk about it anymore..."

"No, no, no. You did great, Yumiko," Wes said jumping up off the table. "That's it!"

"What's it?" Yumiko asked now confused.

Wes began pacing back in forth in front of the boards. "This person knows just like I do that people have short memories. Whatever statement he or she is trying to make would just get lost in the media circus and be quickly forgotten by the next big news story. The killer wants these particular people involved to know something. But what?"

"I don't know Wes. This all points to a second generation Al-Qaeda fringe group. They're testing their genetic weapon before holding the world hostage," Yumiko said doubting Wes.

"Take a step back and think about it, Yumiko. You said the victim, Flora," Wes said pointing at her photo, "died six months ago. Why would a terrorist target a twelve year old girl? And in six months no one else has been attacked until now?"

"You've got a good point but there could be other victims in other cities. Hell, other countries," Yumiko said.

"Okay, let me put it to you like this. International terrorists have trouble making anthrax. Compared to this, making anthrax is like making a peanut butter and jelly sandwich. Maybe one percent of the world's scientist's would have access to the equipment or be able to process a genetic weapon, much less understand it.

"Me, you and maybe a handful of people in the world could do something like this. After the domestic anthrax terrorist attack, you guys must keep track of people with knowledge like this. Is there an onsite database?" Wes insisted.

"This way," Yumiko said striding out of the room as Wes followed.

"It's in the Scientific Criminal Investigation section," Yumiko said rounding a corner.

They went through a set of double doors and down another hallway. A bank of computers were scattered about the room they finally entered. An analyst was seated in front of one of the computers with his back to them. They could hear faint sounds of alternative rock coming from the iPod earbuds stuck in his ears.

Yumiko tapped the analyst on his shoulder and he nearly jumped out of his chair.

"Whoa, what're you trying to do, give me a heart attack?" the analyst asked as he pulled out his earbuds and shut off his iPod.

"Sorry, didn't mean to sneak up on you like that, Martin. We're working on something and we need your help for a minute," Yumiko replied. "Oh, yeah, Wes, Martin, Martin, Wes."

The two men nodded their acknowledgement of each other.

Martin pulled at his goatee for a moment and then said, "Well, I was about to log off and call it a day but what the hell, shoot."

"Can you get information on anyone who is or was working on military government projects and has an advanced degree in genetics, molecular biochemistry and the like in, let's say, the past ten years?" Wes asked.

Martin proceeded to enter the query into the FBI database. After a few moments, the screen came back with thumbnail pictures and profiles of about twenty scientists. Interestingly enough, Wes' name was at the top of the list which Martin happily pointed out.

"Hey, you're in here," Martin said smiling.

"Yeah, see I told you," Wes said to Yumiko and laughed.

Yumiko didn't join the laughter. She frowned instead and then pulled out her cell phone and pressed the walkie-talkie feature. Into the phone she asked, "You there, Gonzalez? Come in."

There was no response so Yumiko punched in another number and pressed the walkie-talkie button again. "Abrams, you there?"

"Yeah, I'm here boss. What's up?" responded Abrams' voice from the phone.

"Martin here is going to send you a list of names, Abrams, of persons of interest," Yumiko said and nodded to Martin who confirmed the order with a nod and began typing away. "I was going to give it to you but find Gonzalez and tell him I want him working that list."

"Okay, I'm on it. And where do you want me?" Abrams responded.

Yumiko said, "I want you to follow up on Dr. Roland Wilhelm."

"Got it. I'll check it out," Abrams said glad that she got the more plum assignment.

"Copy that," Yumiko said and closed her phone.

Wes looked more closely at the profiles and said, "Why isn't Dr. Wilhelm on this list?"

"Is he dead? Because I only queried for living persons. Do you want me to check for deceased scientists, too?" Martin asked.

Seeing where Wes was going Yumiko suggested that they cross-reference the current list against Dr. Wilhelm and any known associates, dead or alive.

After a few moments, the database came back with thumbnails of nine profiles.

"You got your degree, in what, '89?" Yumiko asked.

"Actually, got my master's then. Why?"

"Well, it must be the curse of the grads because a few of your former colleagues are dead."

"Yeah, you're right," Wes said taking a second look at the screen. He noted that four of the people in the profiles were in fact dead. He also noted that they had received advanced degrees around the same time as he. "Please tell me that that's just a coincidence."

"If it'll make you feel better, okay, it's just a coincidence," Yumiko said smiling. "But seriously, Wes, there's obviously something a little deeper than anyone thought going on here. You may want to grow some eyes in the back of your head. If you feel you need some personal security when you're not in the building, let me know."

Standing in front of the board back at the meeting room, Yumiko asked, "Why not the adults?" Yumiko pointed to the photos of Senator Cole and Roland Wilhelm that she had put up.

"Punishment?" Wes asked with a raised eyebrow from the table he was sitting on.

"Or revenge?" Yumiko asked as she picked up a marker and proceeded to draw the outline of a head on the board to the right. In the center of the head she drew a question mark. Above the head, she wrote, "terrorist", "scientist", and "male". Underneath the head she wrote, "female child" and "sick/suffer".

Wes nodded approvingly.

Yumiko tapped the board with the dry-erase pen and said, "Perhaps he had a child that suffered in some way before dying. And he's blaming them for..."

She turned and looked at Wes who could only shrug and stifle a yawn with his fist.

"Ah hell... Now you've got me doing it," Yumiko said as she dropped the pen back into the whiteboard's cradle. "We should be focusing on the cure. There is no one armed man, Wes."

Wes and Yumiko paused for a moment and then broke up laughing.

When the giggles finally subsided and they had wiped the tears from their eyes, Yumiko said, "It's late and we've been at this all day. We're starting to get punchy. Let's get some rest. We'll start early in the morning."

As they gathered their things to leave, Wes paused and said, "One thing though. We are working on the cure. If we can understand the way these people or this person thinks... their motivation, then we'll understand the method. Everyone puts their signature on what they do. Scientists, madmen, artists, it doesn't matter.

"Once we recognize the signature, we'll be that much closer to the cure."

Sunday — December 5th

In the locker room outside of the showers, Wes was just finishing tying his shoes when Yumiko walked in. He had spent the early morning in the lab to see if he could add anything to their progress. He'd been working with live samples and although the chance of catching anything was remote he'd gone through decontamination and a shower anyway.

"So, how is it looking, Wes?" Yumiko asked. "From my morning briefing, it seems like they're on the right track but the computer simulations still break down. The simulations indicate we'll able to slow the disease down but we'd be unable to completely purge it with our current treatment."

Wes stood up from the bench and threw his shower towel into the laundry basket. "Well, reversing genetic manipulation is supposed to be my specialty but I can't see it. There's something strangely familiar about this disease, though. It's on the edge of my mind but it's like the more I look at it, the farther it slips away.

"My first idea was to introduce more manipulation to make the cells that have turned into bone turn back into muscle. The problem there, though, is that it's like putting a layer of paint over another without properly sanding first."

"There'd be underlying bone that would grow back," Yumiko suggested.

"Exactly," Wes said.

"Well, Gonzalez and Abrams are waiting for us, they just back from an interview. They said they've got some interesting and puzzling information for us. We're ready when you are."

"Ready. I need a cup of tea so I'm going to stop by the cafeteria on the way, if you don't mind."

Agent Gonzalez and Abrams were sitting at a large round table in the middle of their meeting room. They had their notes and coffees laid out in front of them as Wes and Yumiko entered.

"G'mornin' Gonzalez, Abrams," Wes said as he put his cup of tea on the table and took a seat. Yumiko sat next to him on his right.

"Mornin'.," Gonzalez and Abrams replied in unison. After having been partners for many years, Gonzalez and Abrams could probably finish each other's sentences.

"You're on, guys," Yumiko said.

Gonzalez went first. He turned to Wes and Yumiko and said, "Initially, last evening when I got that list, I jumped on it quick. I hoped for a quick catch. I know, doubtful, but it happens."

Everyone nodded and he continued. "So, anyway, it turned out that most of those names were dead ends. Pretty much all those scientists still work for the government in one way or another. Even when they're not directly working for the government, they still are through subsidiary companies. They're constantly in for polygraph's and psych evaluations. No way any of them did this.

"I even checked you out, Wes. There were a lot of

blank spots in your work history due to its classified nature, but the Deputy Director cleared me to take a peek. And again, except for a parking ticket or two, nothing."

Wes looked at Yumiko with raised eyebrows. She shrugged as if to say, "Everybody's a suspect, until they're not."

"The bottom line, though," Gonzalez went on, "is that no one, including Wes had any *time* to pull this kind of thing off. From what I've been told by the science staff, it would take a team of them a few years working in a state of the art lab to do it. For a single individual, it would take double the time and a whole lot of private money; millions of dollars, in fact."

"I guess we're back to your terrorist theory, Yumiko," Wes said.

"The only way seems to be a rogue government supporting this kind of work," Yumiko said.

"Not necessarily," Gonzalez interjected. "The research men and women I spoke with said it would be a Herculean task, but not impossible. I'm still checking to see if there were any unusual purchases of the equipment and resources necessary to do this. When Abrams is done with her report, you'll understand why."

He sipped his coffee and looked at Abrams giving her, her cue.

She took a sip of her coffee, cleared her throat and said, "Well, as Yumiko instructed, I followed up on the Wilhelms; Flora and her father Roland.

"Flora died on June 15th according to the final death certificate and doctor's report. Our coroner and forensics people indicate that it took between seven and ten days for the disease to run its course. I checked with the Patient A team and they're not sure about the incubation period for this genetic weapon, but we believe Flora was infected sometime between June 5th and June 7th."

Wes thought about Alex. She had first presented symptoms about a week ago.

"Anything significant about that timeframe?" Yumiko asked.

"We've got an analyst crunching those dates as we speak," Gonzalez replied. "But nothing so far."

Yumiko nodded for Abrams to continue.

"For the five years prior to his daughter's death, Roland was the head of research and development for Gene Therapy Technologies. The company, based in San Mateo County in the California bay area, worked on stem cell and pharmaceutical research. They had a lot of government support due to contacts Dr. Wilhelm established from years spent with the military. And, yes, I did try to check into what he was doing for the military," Abrams said smiling at Yumiko, "but it turns out he was working for military intelligence. All they'd tell me is that it was national security. I've got a request in to the Deputy Director to pry open some doors but so far, zilch."

Impressed and nervous, Wes whistled. "Man, where have I heard that before. Here we go down that rabbit hole again, Alice."

"I know," Abrams said, "and it gets better." Abrams consulted her notes for a moment and then continued.

"Last night, I spoke to a Dr. Franklin, who was Wilhelm's Director of Research. He indicated that on June 17th, Wilhelm stopped by the office. It was about seven in the morning and the rest of the staff hadn't arrived, yet. He had told Dr. Franklin that he came by to pick up a few things to work on at home as he'd be out about a week, maybe two, for the funeral and bereavement back in Maryland. He also had wanted to give Dr. Franklin and the staff some last minute instructions as well.

"Franklin offered his sympathies and then remembered that a package had been delivered the previous day for Dr. Wilhelm. He had left it for Wilhelm on his desk."

Yumiko scratched her head and adjusted her hair before saying, "How was Dr. Franklin able to remember all this so clearly?"

Abrams smiled, "Because of what happened next.

"Sure, Wilhelm had been devastated by his daughter's death. And he had been a widower for many years. It had been he and his daughter for the longest. But Franklin said that when Wilhelm opened that package, he totally lost it. Wilhelm screamed at the top of his lungs and threw the box across the room. Franklin heard something like glass crunch against the wall.

"Dr. Franklin said in all the years he had known him, Dr. Wilhelm had never lost his temper or raised his voice. Not once. Wilhelm apologized for his outburst and quickly left. He didn't bother taking anything with him or leave the instructions as he had planned."

Abrams paused to let this sink in and then went on. "Now get this, Dr. Franklin said that he didn't mean to be nosy, but he went into Wilhelm's office and took a peek at what was inside that package. On the desk was an empty box. Lying on the floor, near the wall was a six-inch tall hourglass with a hole cracked in it. He said it looked well crafted and expensive with hand-carved natural wood supports. Some of the hourglass sand had spilled from the crack out onto the floor."

"A message," Wes said.

"Yes," Yumiko agreed, "but what does it mean?"

"Yeah, I've been thinking about that," Gonzalez said. "Something like, 'hey, mofo, you're outta time'."

Wes stretched and then said, "But if that's the case, why not send him an expensive broken Rolex? Same message, right?"

Gonzalez shrugged.

Yumiko said, "Now we've got to start in on the whole staff of the Gene Therapy company as potential suspects. With every answer we get, we find two more questions. If Alex dies, will Senator Cole get an hourglass, too?"

That question was greeted with silence.

"Well, speaking of the hourglass," Gonzalez said, "after Abrams here gave me the brief rundown, I spoke to Flora's funeral director by phone this morning. And there's more weird stuff.

"Before the hourglass incident, the doctor had made arrangements for his daughter to be buried with her mother. The funeral was scheduled for that Sunday the 20th but Roland went to the funeral director's home the night of the 17th and told the director he wanted his daughter cremated, immediately."

Wes suddenly stood up and started to slowly pace back and forth.

Gonzalez stopped and looked from Yumiko to Wes and back again. Yumiko nodded for him to proceed.

"The director protested due to the late hour, but Dr. Wilhelm wouldn't go away and insisted. Believing Dr. Wilhelm to be insane with grief, the funeral director eventually relented.

"Wilhelm wanted to go along to the funeral

home's crematorium and oversee the procedure himself. I don't mean to put his daughter in the cremator or anything, but he wanted to make sure it was her and watch her body cremated. It was like he didn't want his daughter's body out of his sight for a second.

"The director wouldn't allow it though and threatened to call the police. Dr. Wilhelm backed off and waited in the home's lounge. The director feeling something was fishy didn't burn up Flora's body. He gave Roland ashes from an old wooden coffin, instead. Roland took them and left."

Abrams flipped through a folder on the table and pulled out a report.

"According to this police report, shortly after the doctor returned home, he sat at his desk in his home office, wrote down his last will and testament, and ate a bullet."

Abrams let that one roll around in everyone's head before she said, "Now my question about that is why would a *doctor* eat a bullet? Here he has access to all kinds of drugs. He could go out as high as a kite. Not even feel a thing. But, no, he eats a bullet."

"That's guilt right there," Gonzalez added. "I swear all these suckers are guilty. My bet was he was trying to punish himself for his daughter's death."

Gonzalez looked for confirmation on their faces but none was forthcoming so he pressed on. "Anyway, one of the things he insisted upon in his will was to be cremated as well and have his ashes promptly scattered. As lawyers handled his estate, *his* body was cremated. When the director heard of Roland's death, he waited for someone to come for Flora's body, but no one ever did so he followed the original instructions and had her buried with her mother himself."

Gonzalez, Abrams and Yamazaki looked around when they heard the door close. They hadn't noticed that Wes had quietly slipped out.

Yumiko got up and went out to track Wes down. She looked up and down the halls for him. She even went into the men's restroom in case he had gotten sick. But she finally found him outside in the parking lot. He was sitting at the end of the lot under a tree, staring up at the clear, morning sky.

"Are you all right?" she asked.

"Yeah, I just needed some air. You know look at the clouds. Started to feel claustrophobic. Like I was gonna pass out or something."

"No, it was my fault. I sometimes forget that even with all you've been through, you're still a civilian. You're not a cop. We can overlook the grisly details because we're all about getting the bad guys. But you, you're just trying to help a friend."

A squirrel paused in front of them for a moment hoping for a bite to eat, but when no food came its way, it scurried up the tree. Yumiko sat down on the grass alongside Wes.

"If you want to go back to your hotel and rest..."

Wes shook his lowered head. "No, I'll be okay. Every second counts. All this talk of death reminds me of how selfish I am. But time heals all wounds, right?"

Yumiko nodded.

Wes' head snapped up. "No, not time."

"What's that?" Yumiko asked.

"Did you ever see Lawrence of Arabia?" Wes asked.

"Of course, hasn't everybody?"

"The Gen-Y kids, probably not, but that's beside the point. You remember the part about the quicksand in the movie?"

"Yeah, vaguely," she said, trying to ferret out his meaning.

"Do you remember why it was so dangerous?"

She shook her head.

Wes' eyes narrowed and he nodded. "Because it was dry. They couldn't tell the difference between the sand and the quicksand. One moment you're standing there, and the next you're gone. I don't think that time was the main message of the hourglass sent to Dr. Wilhelm. I think it had something to do with the sand and the Middle East. Maybe you were, right after all, Yumiko."

"Yeah, I can see that. If you're a terrorist or someone from that part of the world with a vendetta, sand is a good metaphor."

They sat contemplating the sky, sand and death for a few minutes when Yumiko's cell phone rang.

"This is Brooks," the Director said when she answered. "General Eric King's daughters have been infected. We need you at his estate right now."

———

Moving from screen to screen, Harold checked the final preparation on his series of computers lined along the wall. Everything was checking out okay. He was five-by, ready to rock-and-roll.

With all the computers there was a slight danger of overheating, but the cool stone and damp air kept the risk under control. The moisture was a problem from time to time and he'd had to replace a part or two, but Harold's business would soon be finished. He just needed the computers to hold out for a few more days.

One of Halli Alfaro's muscle genes spun on the computer screen. A software program adapted by

Harold was adding the final touches to the serum before the actual automated production would begin in the other sealed off 'wet' containment room.

The aerosolized form of the serum in the dust had been particularly time and resource consuming. Although more dangerous for his own personal safety, he decided that he was running out of time and would just go the tried and true hypodermic needle route for his last two victims.

Harold felt like the Abominable Dr. Phibes. Vincent Price was great as the doctor in that movie. Only in the movie, Dr. Phibes had sought revenge of a perceived wrong against his wife. In Harold's case it was for his daughter. Also Dr. Phibes used Egyptian rituals to carry out his justice but Harold had marked his victims with a genetic weapon. Dr. Phibes' way would probably be more satisfying but the world also needed to know about Project Quicksand.

He left his computers and walked down the short metal corridor to his makeshift living room.

The television was on and tuned to Channel 8's Action news. On the screen was an African-American, female reporter. She was standing outside the police tape in front of ex- General King's estate giving an update. She indicated that Channel 8 news had no idea what was happening inside other than the FBI was investigating. Her news station had been informed of the intense FBI activity by an anonymous tip.

"I wonder who that could have been?" Harold asked out loud to the reporter. "Oh, that's right, it was me."

He laughed bitterly as he watched the field agents moving back and forth in their Tyvek bioterrorism suits. Just then the camera followed two more FBI cars as they pulled up at the gate and were quickly let into the estate. The pillbox was being manned by an FBI agent now instead of his good buddy, William.

Harold could tell that three of them running up the walkway were feds, but the fourth, an African-American gentleman, looked out of place; his tan sport-coat stood out like a sore thumb. The news camera refocused on the reporter so Harold had to lean in a little closer to look at the small figure in the background.

"I've seen him before," Harold said pursing his lips as the reporter droned on. "But where?"

It was on the tip of his tongue but just when he almost had it, he was distracted. The robotic arms started whirring and buzzing when they came to life in the sealed production containment room. The computer was done with its analyses and the serum was now being produced.

He wondered if he should begin the production sequence for Serena's genetic markers right away. He had her DNA sample stored and ready to go. He couldn't decide. For some reason, he felt jumpy and a little nervous after seeing that agent or whoever he was on the screen. He turned back to the story but the Channel 8 Action news had moved on to sports.

"I guess I'm only worth three minutes," Harold said. "For now, anyway. When the whole story comes out, it'll be something that's going to shake the foundations of the world for years to come."

He got up to go and check on the serum production. Now what was that guy's name? he asked himself. Don't worry, he answered himself. It'll come to you. It'll come.

Feeling like a little kid as the grown folks talked, Wes milled about the living room waiting for Yumiko and Brooks to finish their huddle.

When they had arrived, the main house had been cordoned off. The bioterrorism unit could still be seen wandering around taking samples in their Tyvek suits but really, the all clear had been sounded about an hour ago.

Wes hadn't particularly liked the news cameras outside. He could just imagine how the harassment would start all over again if someone got wind of who he was. Maybe Brooks was right that he would be a detriment to the case. Next time he saw any cameras; Wes decided he'd slip in through the back.

Eric King, the former Army general in charge of Middle East operations, entered the living room and joined the huddle.

Wes was blessed with keen ears and a sharp nose. They made up for his poor vision. As such, although they spoke in hushed tones, he easily overheard Eric tell Brooks, that Mrs. King was still at the University of Maryland's Hospital with the girls. Ever since the morning when Tiana hadn't been able to wake her sister, Charlene King had never left their side. Not in the ambulance and not at the hospital where they identified the disease and not now. The identification interview regarding the suspect would just have to wait, she had said.

Finally the huddle broke up and the Director beckoned Wes over.

Quick introductions were made and then Brooks said, "What we know so far is that it was a lone individual masquerading as a children's party clown. Copies of the surveillance tapes and home videos have been sent to headquarters and Annex B. You

can view them later. For now, we want everyone to
take a look at this particular video that was recorded
by one of the guests."

Brooks nodded to an agent who turned on the
plasma screen television and the DVD player. The
picture showed a freeze frame image of a clown in
the middle of a somersault.

"We believe the perpetrator was unaware that he
was being filmed as this party guest only began
recording midway through his act. We're not sure if
he had taken this into account or if it even factored
into his plans. Regardless, we want to use the video
to ID this fiend," Brooks said.

The tape was paused at various points as Brooks
lobbed questions at Yumiko, Abrams and Gonzalez.
They'd worked counter-terrorism for years and
Brooks wanted to know if they knew him. Does
anyone recognize him? Does his M.O. look familiar?
How about his height? His weight? The eyes or the
shape of the nose? Come on, people! Anything?
Anything at all.

Unfortunately, none of them were familiar with
him. The man *did* seem familiar to Wes though. He
couldn't quite place from where. And is it my
imagination or does it sound as if the Director is
trying to make sure we *don't* recognize the
individual, Wes thought.

"Now let's go back to the point where he infects
them with the dust," the Director ordered. The agent
complied and set the video image to the point where
the clown had just spun the dust into the air.

The video rolled forward in slow motion. The
camera had been focused on the two girls at that
time.

Yumiko said, "Yes, we can clearly see them
sneezing. But was that a reaction to the dust in

general or the genetic weapon?"

Wes said, "Well, I didn't see anyone else sneezing. But I doubt, if this is the same FOP genetic weapon, that sneezing would have anything to do with the disease anyway."

"Then perhaps an initial marker to make sure that the infection hit the right target," Yumiko suggested. "Have you ever seen anything like this, General King?"

Director Brooks glared at Yumiko but she ignored him. The former general shook his head in response to the question.

A palpable tension seemed to settle into the room until Gonzalez broke it with, "Hey, did you guys see that? There as the camera quickly panned across the room!"

Everyone peered closer at the screen. During the party the camera person had quickly whipped across the room after the dust had settled. The clown's reaction had been filmed for just a split second. The agent manning the image, rolled it back to the clown frame by frame.

Abrams said, "That sick bastard. He's..."

"...smiling," Gonzalez finished.

Eric punched the wall in anger and the whole room shook. Although retired military, he was still able to use his fist with his six-foot two inch frame behind it to put a nice hole in the living room wall.

Everyone knew exactly how he felt so no one remarked on the punch. Instead, Brooks said, "Sick but smart, too. We have of course gone over the whole home with a fine tooth comb, but the floor samples were the most interesting."

"What did we find?" Yumiko asked.

"Nothing."

Brooks let that sink in and then continued,

"Somehow, that we've yet to determine, unless this weapon is inserted and active in a living host within a certain amount of time, it breaks down into its natural elemental components."

"He hides his tracks well. Just another cowardly killer," Gonzalez said.

Wes shook his head. "I don't think so. I think it's to guard against cross-contamination. The weapon obviously has genetic markers from samples of the victim's own DNA but he wants to make sure that only the victims are harmed. No innocent victims from accidental exposure."

"But how did he get my little girls' DNA?" Eric asked.

"Unfortunately all too easy," volunteered Abrams. "He could've gone through your trash and gotten hair samples from a brush. Or maybe a saliva sample from something they had recently eaten..."

"Wait!" yelled the bodyguard who had been quietly sitting unobserved a few feet away.

"Do you have a problem?" asked the Director. "Aren't you one of the bodyguards who were assigned to protect the girls? I thought we relieved you of duty after debriefing, Ms. Thompson. What're you still doing here?"

"I'm sorry, sir, but I've been with those girls and this family for years. I feel like it's my fault and I wanted to do something, anything to help," the security guard Thompson said.

"Well, you've done enough, you can go," Brooks said with a sneer.

"Now hold on a second..." Eric King began before Yumiko cut him off.

"Will you both shut up for a minute? She's trying to tell us something."

Thompson smiled at Yumiko and nodded. She

ran a restless hand through her tied-back brown hair and took a deep breath.

"Okay, take your time and tell us what's wrong," Yumiko said.

"Well, when agent Abrams there mentioned eaten, I remembered something. When your people interviewed me earlier I couldn't remember ever having seen the perpetrator before but I think I do now. I was so shocked before that I couldn't think straight.

"Yesterday morning, when we were at the park, there was a man there. He was eating a muffin. That's what jogged my memory; when you mentioned eating something. Anyway, at the time, myself and Parks, the other security officer, kind of wrote him off as any kind of threat. But now, I'm pretty sure that it was him. His build and the graceful way he moved were the same. He must've been doing reconnaissance at the park."

"What?" Brooks said, angrily. "You're only telling us this now! We've got ten federal agents scouring the tri-state area looking for a white van. We've got another ten checking party shops for recent purchases. Now you're telling me we've been wasting all this time because you could ID this guy but conveniently forgot to mention it?"

Wes looked at Yumiko and the other agents. They were all taken aback at Brooks' outburst. His tirade was uncalled for given the bodyguard's obvious emotional attachment to the girls. Yes, everyone wanted to get to the bottom of the incident but not by berating and humiliating someone who already felt like dirt.

Brooks realized that everyone was staring at him so in a more even tone he said, "I'm taking Thompson down to Annex B with me right now to work up a sketch with our forensic artist. Yumiko, you take your team down to that park and get me everything you can."

He then grabbed the security officer's arm and abruptly walked out of the room with her. Eric King quickly followed after them.

Yumiko and her team all looked at each other. Wes watched the fascinating thing called cop telepathy at work for a few seconds. Wes could imagine what they were saying to each other: Did you see that? That was nuts. Maybe he's under pressure from the higher-ups. Then Yumiko said, "All right. You heard the man, let's go."

Sitting outside of and down the street a bit from Halli Alfaro's apartment, Harold considered his options.

He sat in his beat-up, red 2004 Toyota pick-up sipping his Java King espresso and thinking. He peeked through his binoculars between sips. He was alternately watching the secret service agents sitting in their sedan down the street and the windows of Halli's apartment.

The King girls had been easy to track and infect because they had bodyguards. Bodyguards are trained to prevent physical harm. Secret service agents on the other hand are trained to *identify* threats before they result in physical harm.

After the Secret Service was folded into the Department of Homeland Security, the former Secretary of Defense, Frank Alfaro had petitioned for and received a new protocol that the Service provide security for his current cabinet position. The protocol also required that he'd get the protection for another five years after leaving his post. If I had made as many enemies as he had, I would've doubled up on my protection too, Harold thought. Unfortunately for Harold, the security for the ex-Secretary extended to his family, too.

He doubted he'd be able to take Halli in the open without getting himself nabbed. He thought about doing the Director's daughter Serena first and then coming back to Halli, but the feds would issue a nationwide manhunt to catch him after Serena. It was a fifty-fifty shot either way that he wouldn't be able to finish his masterpiece.

"No, I better just stick to the plan. All I need is one small opening," Harold said to himself. "And, besides, I want Brooks to really sweat. I want him to know I'm coming and sweat under the fear that he won't be able to stop it. Just like I had to sweat."

Harold picked up the scanner's headphones from the passenger seat and put them on. He flipped through the channels on the scanner for the bugs he had planted in Halli's apartment.

Back at the end of August he had gotten into her three-bedroom apartment posing as a utility worker. The landlord hadn't even looked twice at his forged job invoice.

Halli and her roommate, Gina Kim, had been away on a Caribbean vacation. He had learned quite a bit about them from exploring their rooms at his leisure. He also picked up some nice DNA samples after he had planted the listening bugs.

He had assumed that soon after Halli's return, the apartment would have been electronically swept. The bugs would have had a short usefulness time. But that never happened. Halli apparently valued her privacy above her safety; especially since she had a hot, steady boyfriend these days. Gina had not been too keen on the idea of letting strangers roam around among her intimate things, either. As a result, the secret service agents weren't allowed to enter the residence and conduct sweeps without Halli's prior permission. The service wasn't easily embarrassed by their charges' sexual forays, but Halli, it seems was. And so, Halli had never let the agents in and Harold's electronic infestation remained.

Gina had already gone out for her study session at the George Washington School of Law, come back and left again. G.W. Law was only five minutes away by car. Gina was in her second year of international law, Halli her first. Final exams were coming up this week.

Harold had followed them both around the G. W. Law campus on more than a few occasions. He had even sat in on one of Halli's classes with her sitting just a few seats away in front of him. He came to the conclusion from her dismal class performance that he was probably doing her a favor by killing her; she was a terrible student.

About half an hour ago, Gina had left the apartment in her work clothes. Halli had had a study session today, too, but he wasn't surprised that she still hadn't gotten up; she'd partied all night. She had skipped a lot of her regular classes, much less a study class.

Just then, Harold heard a loud yawn and rustling over his headphones. Halli was finally awake.

He heard her mumble something to herself as she got up and shuffled off and into the bathroom. Switching to the mike in the bathroom, Harold could clearly hear Halli relieving herself; that universal tinkling sound of water on porcelain. He heard the toilet paper roll spin. Then, she wiped herself and flushed the toilet. She washed her hands and exited the bathroom.

Continuing to flip through the channels for the various listening devices as Halli moved between rooms, Harold followed Halli's morning routine.

After she had finished her cereal brunch and threw on some clothes, Halli had plopped down on her sofa and turned on the television. Having gone through her wardrobe, Harold could imagine her laying there wearing a grey G. W. sweatshirt and sweatshorts.

She ran her remote up and down the satellite channels. Her loud sigh indicated that she didn't seem to find anything worth watching. She switched the television off and grabbed her cell phone. She quickly punched in some numbers. Harold could guess who she was calling.

"Hi, Kurt, whatcha doing?" Halli whispered into the phone.

She listened for a few minutes, laughed and asked, "Well then, why don't you come over?"

Harold and Halli waited for the answer. Finally, she asked, "You're going to go to work on Sunday again? How long do you have to be at the firm?"

While they waited again, Harold made sure the automatic voice recorder plugged into the scanner had in fact activated. He adjusted the volume a bit and checked on the secret service with his binoculars. They hadn't moved. From what Harold could tell, they were eating snacks and surfing the internet. Then, Halli said, "Oh, that's too bad. Well, do they need you to do more research on that case tomorrow? We can go see Twilight Dance down at The Rialto."

Another pause and then, "Exams? I don't have

an exam tomorrow. Mine are later in the week."

Harold knew that that statement was a lie. Harold knew Halli's school schedule like it was his own and she had a 10:00 a.m. civil law exam on Monday. He was surprised Kurt was unfamiliar with her schedule. But then again, maybe he did know. It wasn't like Kurt was dating her for her brains.

Again the pause and then Halli said, "Oh, them? I know you hate it. Me, too. But don't worry, I know how to ditch them when I need to. I've done it before..."

Kurt and Halli continued talking but Harold had zoned out. He'd listen again to the recorded version later. For now, his mind was going over the words, "I know how to ditch them" again and again. Already a plot was taking shape in Harold's mind and his face was, of course, smiling.

"What're we doing out here, boss?" Suzette called out across the park to Yumiko. "I mean I seriously doubt we're going to find anything. That van's probably gonna be found burnt up in some parking lot somewhere."

Twilight had come to the park. Deep shadows flooded the grounds around the trees. In the dimming daylight the children's slide looked like an ancient dinosaur.

As Yumiko passed the beam of her flashlight back and forth along the ground searching, she replied, "You heard Brooks. He wants us to at least make a good faith effort. He got caught with his pants down in front of King back at the estate. I'm sure he doesn't want any blowback. You know, CYA. These *are* the daughters of a former army general we're talking about here."

"I don't know, Yamazaki," Gonzalez called out from over by the garbage bin, which he had opened and had been carefully digging through. "I'm gonna have to go with Abrams on this one. We're the lead on this investigation. We should be back at headquarters getting the first crack at the visual ID. The B team should be out here going through the trash, not the A team."

Yumiko held back her laugh as she continued her methodical search of the sandbox area. Then she called out, "All right. One more sweep and then we're outta here. Gonzalez, let Wes know."

Gonzalez glanced over at Wes who was leaning against the trunk of one of their sedans. Wes' face was illuminated by the cell phone pressed to his ear. Gonzalez could hear the faint sounds of Wes' voice. Poor guy, Gonzalez thought as he went back to sifting through the trash bin.

"Well, the drug cocktail seems to be working as far as her lungs are concerned. That's good news because we've been able to sit her up and talk to her. The bad news is that the ossification of her heart tissue is still proceeding unchecked," Senator Cole said.

"Yeah, I've been getting reports on the effectiveness of the cocktail. But now we've at least got some sort of suspect, Janet. We're out here right now at the park where he was seen yesterday, looking for evidence. When we catch this guy, we'll be able to get the info on how he did this and cure Alex," Wes declared.

Sounds of an ambulance could be heard in Senator Cole's background getting closer to the hospital as she said, "Oh, my gosh. I pray that you can find this person. My poor baby doesn't deserve this."

"Don't worry, we will. These guys I'm out here with are good; especially, lead agent, Yamazaki. She's scary smart. Actually, she was going to talk to you about something," Wes said as an idea suddenly came to him.

"Oh, about what?"

Wes toed a pebble with his foot for a few seconds as he thought about how to phrase the question. He decided on the direct route and said, "In the course of the investigation today, we ran across the name of a Roland Wilhelm. Have you ever heard of this person before?"

"No, I've never heard of him before. Why? Is he important to the case? If he is, I could check my records or something," Senator Cole said without missing a beat.

"I just hoped you knew something off the top of your head, but it's okay. If the investigators really want you to look into it, I'm sure they'll let you know," Wes said hoping his words didn't sound hollow or forced since his mind was now elsewhere.

"When will I get to see the artist's rendition of the suspect? I want to see the bastard's face who did this to my little girl."

"I'm not sure that's really such a good idea, Janet. You may be tempted to get your own brand of justice, but it's not really my call. I'll let you know when they've got it, at least," Wes offered before saying goodbye and ending the call.

Gonzalez came over when he saw Wes was done and told him they were packing up their stuff and would be leaving shortly. All Wes could do was nod. Gonzalez looked at him quizzically and then walked off to join Abrams and Yamazaki.

She lied to me about Wilhelm, Wes thought as

the team packed their gear away in the cars. He sensed it the moment the words left her lips. But, why?

In the car, as the amber city lights flickered past Wes' face, he kept turning the conversation over and over in his mind. Yumiko turned from observing the road and said, "You've been kind of quiet. Bad news or something?"

"Yeah, I guess you could say that," he replied as he stared at the night. "Oh, but Alex is still hanging in there so it's not all bad news. There's something else that I can't quite put my finger on."

"Well, do you want to bounce it off me?"

"I'd like to but there's really nothing there, yet. Just a feeling that there's a lot more going on here than people are letting on. But I'll let you know when I've got something. How about on your end? Anything?" Wes asked finally turning to look at Yumiko directly.

Stopped at a red light, they could clearly see drizzle starting to come down.

"There was nothing at the park. Didn't really expect there would be. If the guy's smart enough to make a genetic weapon, I doubt he's worried about leaving trace evidence at a crime scene. Hell, he probably took someone else's DNA and planted it at the scene just so we'll look foolish busting down some poor, innocent sucker's door. That's what I'd do," Yumiko said as the light changed and she eased forward.

Wes smiled and shook his head.

"What?" Yumiko asked smiling herself.

"Nothing. I'd hate to be a criminal if you were chasing me is all."

"Damn straight," she said nodding. "Anyway, when we get back to Annex B, we're going to run the sketch of this guy through our Facial Recognition Imaging System, if Brooks hasn't started already. We should know who this asshole is in a few hours, if not less.

"You know, I didn't agree with all the data mining stuff they pulled several years ago, but every once and a while when we've got an actual terrorist, it's useful. Truth be told, our database has over 500 million profiles in it. Over half of which are Americans."

Wes whistled. "That's almost the entire U.S. population."

"Yeah, we'll get this guy. No problem."

After they had parked and gone through security check, Yumiko, with Wes and her team in tow, made a beeline straight for the Forensics Section in the back of the first floor. Once there, they made their way down a long aisle towards Christina Phan's desk.

Christina waved when she saw them and said to Yumiko, "Hey, stranger what are you doing back here in no man's land?"

"Getting you back on my team, Agent Phan," Yumiko teased.

"Yeah, right," Christina said laughing. "I'm fine right where I am, thank you very much."

"So, where's Brooks? I thought he'd be here," Yumiko said turning to the business at hand.

"No, he left about half an hour ago. Said he was going back to J. Edgar."

"And the sketch?" Gonzalez asked.

"He took that with him. Didn't even bother to run it through F.R.I.S. either. When I asked him about it, he said he wanted to take an image capture of the clown and compare them to make sure he had the right person, first."

"And what about the security guard? I think, Thompson, was her name. Where'd she go?" Suzette asked.

"Brooks told her she could go when she was done."

The team, Wes included, all looked to Yumiko. An almost imperceptible shake of Yumiko's head told them: Don't talk about it now, we'll discuss this later.

Phan reading the telepathy said, "See? That's why I left. All the crazy infighting and one-upmanship. Brooks is going to save the day and take all the credit, while the boots on the ground get screwed again, right? Anyway, I guess it's lucky for you I made another copy."

Phan motioned for them to follow her back into the media lab.

"When I was done with the sketch and Brooks had the original, although he'd watched me the whole time, asked me if I had made any other copies. I said of course not and he left," Phan said as she logged into her computer. "I thought that was a little strange, like somebody was trying to snake someone so I came back here and produced another drawing from memory before I forgot. I'm sure it's missing some things from the first drawing I made but it's close enough. It'll hold up in court for an ID."

Phan used her mouse and clicked in a few places on her screen. A moment later a full screen image of an African-American man's face appeared. "I scanned the sketch into a file folder on a separate drive from where media files are usually kept, just in case."

"You did good, Phan. You did good. But then you always did," Yumiko said smiling at her old partner.

"Should I run it through F.R.I.S.?" Phan asked.

"Yep, let's do it," Yumiko replied as she reached for her cell phone.

Phan called up the program, logged in and input the image for comparison.

As everyone watched, images on the right side of the screen whipped by as they were compared to the suspect's reference image on the left.

Keeping one eye on the screen, Wes sidled over to Yumiko. He said, "Do you remember when we were looking at those profiles of scientists with links to Dr. Wilhelm?"

"Way ahead of you, Wes," Yumiko said as she snapped her cell phone shut. "I recognized him, too. This guy was one of those scientists; one of the dead ones. I just left a message for Martin to send that same info down here to us."

They all watched as the images on the right continued to flash by until finally one stopped. It was almost the exact match to the drawing on the left; the same image of the African-American face but now in life-like detail. The F.R.I.S. picture also showed a younger man. However, all the personal information fields from the F.R.I.S. entry had the word 'classified' entered next to them. Name: Classified, Age: Classified, Occupation: Classified, and so on down the list.

Then there was a loud beep and a flashing message in red popped up in the center of the screen. It said: Security Clearance Required to View this File. A couple seconds later, the screen went blank and another message appeared which read: This log on information has been traced and forwarded. Please contact your supervisor immediately.

Phan said, "Oh shit. See, this is why..."

But she was cut-off by Yumiko's ringing cell

phone. Yumiko flipped it open and listened. She mouthed the words, "It's Martin," and continued to listen.

"Yep, the same thing happened to us," Yumiko said into the phone.

She listened for a moment more before saying, "All right, thanks anyway for trying, Martin."

She flipped the phone closed and said to her team, "Same thing happened to Martin when he was trying to retrieve the list from yesterday. Man, this is not good. I think we should..."

But before she could finish her sentence, her cell phone rang again. Yumiko flipped it open and her eyes slowly became as big as saucer plates as she listened.

The rest of them could hear faint sounds of yelling coming from the phone. Yumiko mouthed the word, "Brooks" as the tongue lashing by him continued.

Finally, the yelling stopped and Yumiko said, "Yes, sir" before closing her phone.

She looked at the group with a steely gaze and shook her head. "We're off the case."

Monday — December 6

Screams woke Wes up from another nightmare. When he sat up, sweat drenched, looking for the source of the screaming he realized that it had been himself. He hoped that his scream hadn't been too loud. He didn't relish a police interview.

Every year around this time he expected to have nightmares over what happened to Chiang-Mei. In fact, in a weird way, he had come to welcome them. He always felt awful and sad but also somehow close to her.

This dream was different though. In this dream, he had been strapped to an operation table. Brooks had loomed over him dressed in an operating gown. He had begun performing experiments on Wes, turning him into one of the creatures Wes had envisioned during the Super Soldier project. Only, the monster Brooks had turned Wes into had been a thousand times worse. And the whole time, Brooks had kept yelling hysterically, "This is what you get when you fuck with me! This is what you get!"

The dream seemed to portend something ominous. Wes shook himself, then got up and put on a robe. It had rained all last night and it was cool.

A loud and long yawn escaped from his mouth.

He sat back down on the side of the bed and glanced at his half-eaten carnitas burrito that was on the nightstand. Even after all that running around yesterday, hearing they had been removed from the case, had effectively killed his appetite. How was he going to save Alex or the twins now?

Wes sat on the bed for awhile longer letting the sleep slough off of him at its leisure. When he was sure he was fully awake, Wes realized his throat felt a bit sore. He hoped he wasn't catching a cold. That's all he'd need.

He got up and went over to the mini-fridge. Usually they only stocked those things with bottled water or soda, but Wes was in luck; there was orange juice. Almost in one draught he drank the plastic pint of juice. It was so sweet and refreshing. He immediately felt better. He tossed the empty plastic bottle into the bin under the nightstand.

Wandering over to the window, Wes looked outside at the gloomy sky and thought, what the hell was that dream with Brooks about? If they didn't want him on the case anymore then that was on them. I should be grateful, Wes thought. They just did me a favor. I have my own loved ones I should be thinking abo...

Wes paused and then shook his head and laughed. "Why didn't I see it before?"

Wes quickly returned to the nightstand and scooped up his cell-phone. He punched in Yumiko's number. Then, he paced as he waited for her to pick up.

"Hello," Yumiko answered.

"Yumiko. Wes. I think I've got it. We've got to get back into headquarters and talk to your friend, Martin."

"Wes, forget about it. We don't have access to

those files anymore."

"No, I'm not looking to find the killer. Well not directly anyway. I'm looking for who the next victim will be."

"Sorry, I haven't had my morning coffee, yet. Back up and run that by me again."

"Okay, sorry. Brooks has a daughter doesn't he?"

There was a long pause before Agent Yamazaki replied.

With understanding in her voice she said, "Yes, yes, he does. I'm such an idiot. That's why he's been acting so weird. He's probably known from the jump that his family was a target. He's been trying to protect them. There never was a middle-eastern terrorist plot. That was smoke and mirrors.

"Like you said, Wes, you and I could maybe pull something like this off. For all he knows, we might be involved. He doesn't know who to trust. There's still something missing, though; the connection. What do Cole, Brooks, Wilhelm, and King all have in common?"

"Exactly," Wes agreed. "That's why we've got to get back to headquarters. We need another peek into those databases."

Yumiko thought for a minute and then said, "Okay, I'll pick you up in twenty."

———————

Harold woke up and yawned. He stretched and sat up on the couch. It was getting more and more uncomfortable, day by day. He'd found it thrown out a few months ago and he'd hauled it back to his makeshift home in the back of his little pickup. He considered getting a new sofa but then thought better of it. "When my mission's complete I won't need anything anymore. Ever," he said to himself.

He tossed off the comforters he'd been sleeping under and got up. He went off to the bathroom and relieved himself before proceeding to his lab.

The small case sitting on the lab table contained two pneumatic high injection hypodermic syringes. They were military issue used in the field during combat. They were especially useful because they could inject a full dose within seconds through thick clothing. It never failed to surprise Harold that he could buy such things so easily on the black market.

After opening the case, he checked the syringes to make sure they were still in working order. Satisfied, he returned them and closed the case. He still needed to transfer the genetic weapon from the containment unit to the syringes, but he'd do that later. What he needed to do now, was make sure he had the architectural plans of the movie theater and the map of the nearby streets, committed to memory.

He went over to his fridge and pulled out a quart of milk. He sipped straight from the carton and walked back over to the couch.

Pulling the coffee table close, he rolled open the blueprint to the theater that was laid on it. He used his milk as a paperweight to keep the paper from curling back up and began to memorize.

―――――――

Once Wes and Yumiko were back at headquarters, Martin balked at the prospect of getting caught again.

"Look, Yumiko, you know I want to help you guys, but this is my career we're talking about here," Martin pleaded. "I just got dragged over the coals. It wasn't fun."

"How long have you known me, Martin?" Yumiko asked rhetorically. "You know I wouldn't ask you but this is life and death here."

Wes added, "I've seen this show before, Martin. These are the big-wigs at the top trying to control this. Put their spin on it for whatever reason. But you can't control someone like this guy. He's not going to stop. More people are going to die."

Martin removed his glasses, rubbed the bridge of his nose and then put his glasses back on. "Okay, okay, I'll do it. Stand back and watch the master work."

His fingers flying over the keys, Yumiko related the info they needed and Martin cross-referenced in an attempt to dig it up.

When his fingers finally stopped, Martin said, "Okay, Brooks, Cole, Wilhelm, King and former Secretary of State Frank Alfaro, all have daughters and they all were involved in and around top secret military intelligence projects about eight years ago. But then again, who wasn't?"

Wes said, "Anybody not involved in secret projects eight years ago, please raise your hand." No one did. Then they all broke out laughing.

Yumiko wiped the tears that had come to her eyes from her giggles and said, "Okay, okay. Let's see what we've got here. Six months ago, Wilhelm's daughter is infected. Then about a week ago, Alexandra Cole is infected. Two days ago, the King twins are infected..."

"He's picking up the pace," Martin added.

Yumiko nodded and then asked Martin, "Did you get that other stuff I asked you about?"

Martin reached into the lower right drawer and pulled out a manila envelope. "Luckily for you, I've still got friends in low places. You owe me big, Yumiko."

"Yeah, yeah," she replied as she took the envelope and opened it. She reached inside and pulled out an 8x10 photo of the man they were seeking. She flipped over the photo and showed Wes the biography that was attached.

"So do you know him?" she asked.

Wes leaned in to read. "I thought at first he was a guy I went to Cal Tech with, but it says here, he went to MIT so he's not the guy I was thinking of. But let's see, his name is Travis Cage. Travis Cage, Travis Cage, sounds familiar."

"When I was researching, I discovered he won a lot of science awards and events," Martin suggested.

Wes thought about that and then said, "Nope, sorry. I'm drawing a blank. Maybe he authored a paper I read somewhere. In any event, he must be pretty smart if he went to MIT.

"Or should I say 'was pretty smart'? 'Cause according to this," Wes said tapping the picture, "he's supposed to be dead. I guess that makes me Fox and you must be Scully."

"This guy's no ghost," Yumiko said. "Did we get how he died, Martin?"

"Yeah, there's a small blurb from a local paper, McLean Connection, in there."

Yumiko pulled out the newspaper article printout from the envelope and read it. She passed it to Wes when she was done.

"About seven year ago the Fairfax police responded to an apparent suicide when Travis Cage drove off a cliff at Great Falls National Park. There was a note found at the scene indicating he was despondent over his wife divorcing him," Wes read.

"If he is alive, do you think he would've

contacted her?" Martin asked.

Yumiko thought about it and then shrugged. "Either way, we'll have to interview her. And we'll have to put 24-hour surveillance on her home and place of business. We need to know what was behind that divorce. And anything else she could tell us about him."

"Like if he had a daughter?" Wes asked.

"Especially that but also what he was doing in the years prior. The article says that he was a lecturing professor," Yumiko replied. "But somehow I doubt that."

"How do we stop him from striking again in the meantime? It looks like Brooks and Alfaro are the only two left on his list, as far as we know. And I doubt they'd let you guys use their daughters as bait. Maybe a young looking agent could impersonate them?" Wes asked.

"Maybe, assuming Cage doesn't already know what they look like" Yumiko said, "but we still have to warn them. Thanks for all your help, Martin. If any heat comes down on you because of this, just tell them I twisted your arm. Brooks has a staff meeting today so he should be here. We'll go up and talk to him. Come on, Wes."

As they made their way to the bank of elevators, Wes said, "Are you sure you want me to tag along? I don't think I'm Brooks most favorite person. I can't figure out what I did to piss him off so much, though."

"Brooks was born pissed off. Probably didn't like the doctor slapping him on the butt. Don't worry about it. I need you to be the objective and reasonable one, to help convince him to let us back in on this. We've got to help those girls."

One of the elevators came to rest on their floor.

They stepped into the elevator. Yumiko pushed the button for Brooks' floor.

Wes asked, "So who do you think is next?"

"You mean Brooks' daughter or Alfaro's?"

Wes nodded the affirmative.

"Well, honestly, my feelings about my boss aside, I'd go after his daughter, Serena, if I was Travis. She's only sixteen. She's an easier target than Halli Alfaro, who's twenty-eight."

"But Alexandra is twenty. How do we resolve that conflict?" Wes opined.

"Good point. There may also be a personal component to his list. If this is about a political statement or revenge, then he may be going down the list in a particular order that coincides with his insanity," Yumiko proposed.

The elevator stopped and they got off. They turned left and proceeded down the long corridor to Brooks' Annex office. The door was ajar and Brooks could be seen walking back and forth. He was talking on his cell-phone.

Yumiko knocked a couple of times and then pushed the door open.

Brooks yelled into the phone, "Hold on! She just showed up. I'll call you back."

Yumiko and Wes entered the office and stood on either side of the front of Brooks' desk.

He hung up, dropped his cell on the desk and then turned to Yumiko. "I thought I told you that you were off the case. You should be at your desk pushing paper. What're you still doing poking around?"

"But, sir," Yumiko insisted, "You have to hear us out."

Yumiko pulled out the photo from her envelope and pointed at it.

"This guy, Travis Cage, is the one behind it all. But more importantly sir, we're pretty confident that your daughter is in danger."

Wes said, "I think you should get your daughter out of town or at least into protective custody, Brooks."

Pointing a finger at Wes' face, Brooks said, "I don't give a fuck what *you* think."

"And as for you," the Director said turning back to Yumiko, "We've known that we might be in danger from day one. Ever since 9/11, every high-level staff member is briefed daily on possible terrorist threats to them personally or otherwise. This includes domestic as well as international terrorists.

"Serena's fine. She's been guarded 24-hours a day by a four man detail since we found out about this."

Shocked, Yumiko said, "Why didn't you tell me?"

"I was going to tell you when I got the clearance to bring you in the loop, but you just couldn't follow orders. You're suspended, Yumiko, until further notice. I've reassigned your team to my daughter's detail. Now give me your badge" Brooks ordered with his hand out.

Yumiko shoved the photo back into the envelope. Too angry to reply, Yumiko bypassed Brooks and slammed her badge down on his desk.

Brooks shook his head and said, "So dramatic, Yumiko. I see you're not carrying at the moment. You'll turn in your firearm to the Sergeant of Arms as soon as possible."

Wes pointed back at Brooks and said, "You're making a mistake."

"As for you, Wes, the only place I want to see you is in the lab, helping us to find a cure. If you can't do that, then you might as well pack your bags. We've studied the files you've given us. We really don't need you anymore. If not for Cole, you'd be gone already. Now get out of my office," Brooks said with a shooing motion.

Wes and Yumiko looked at each other for a moment, decided that it was useless to argue any further and then left.

They were quiet as they walked back down the corridor towards the elevators. Yumiko was thinking about what her father would have done. He'd have probably punched Brooks in the jaw and laid him out cold. Her father didn't take shit off of nobody. He was tough as nails.

Yumiko was tough, too. She had fired her weapon with lethal intent on a couple of occasions and hadn't thought twice before pulling the trigger. But she was a woman. She knew that Brooks would've liked nothing better than to kick her off the Bureau permanently. And swinging at him would've given him an easy out.

Wes was thinking about Alex lying somewhere in a hospital bed. He could imagine each breath getting harder and harder for her as her lungs slowly petrified. He could almost see the beating of her heart becoming more and more erratic as muscle turned to bone.

They'd never find the cure in time. All of the girls would be dead by then. He had to find this guy and his lab and get the cure. He was sure the killer had it.

When the elevator arrived, they stepped inside and Wes pushed the button for the lobby.

Wes turned to Yumiko and said, "So, what now?"

"Well, I'm going to interview the ex-wife of course," she said smiling. "Brooks is wrong. I'm going to find out what's really going on and make him eat his words."

Wes laughed and clapped Yumiko on the shoulder. "Man, you're something else."

"Yep and don't forget it. How about you?" Yumiko asked.

"I guess I'll go back to the hotel and work on the cure. I've got the laptop and the PDA," he said.

Yumiko looked at him sideways. "Yeah, right, Wes. Look I don't know what you're up to, but don't do anything stupid. This guy's dangerous. Don't go looking for him. You let me handle that. Besides, if I find anything out, I may need to bounce it off you. We're a pretty good team."

"Hey, don't worry about me. I'm afraid of my own shadow. I'll just be doing some research," Wes said.

Again she looked at him skeptically but the elevator had just stopped so she dropped the issue. The doors opened and they stepped out.

"Do you need a ride back to your hotel?"

"No, first I think, I'll maybe head down to the lab and check on their progress. Catch up on anything I've missed. New theories, trials, etc.," Wes answered.

"Okay, I'll call you later," she said and strode off.

Wes watched her go. He caught himself admiring her figure and admonished himself under his breath. "No time to be thinking that stuff, Wes."

He headed in the direction of the lab, but stopped short of actually going in. He bent down and feigned tying a shoe. He was making sure Yumiko hadn't backtracked to check on him. When he was sure he went back to see Martin.

"So, what happened with Brooks?" Martin asked.

"He threw a little tantrum but other than that it was okay," Wes lied. "But, hey, Yumiko's waiting for me. She just wanted me to come back and confirm the address for Halli Alfaro."

Wes waited as Martin called up the information and printed it out for him. "Thanks," Wes said grabbing the printout and left.

Yumiko had been pretty confident that Serena would be next, but Wes' instincts told him that Halli would be the one. He didn't know how he knew. Somewhere from the deep dark recesses of his mind the answer had floated up to him.

Outside, Wes walked to the end of the block and hailed a cab. He'd rent a car and go stake out Halli's place. He only hoped that he wasn't already too late.

Travis Cage a.k.a Harold Smith put the final touches on his disguise. He looked at himself in the mirror and admired his work.

A threadbare, knit cap was pulled down over his ears. White tufts from the wig he was wearing poked out from underneath it.

Since he had infected the twins, he had let his beard and mustache grow. Scruffy salt and pepper hair covered his face.

He had done a good job of making himself look like a senior citizen. Perhaps, he was an old, retired widower; someone who spent his afternoons catching a show now and again to kill time.

Reaching into the inner pockets of the old overcoat he'd donned, he made sure the syringes on either side were loaded and secure.

He stepped out of the bathroom and grabbed a manila envelope resting on the coffee table. Then, he moved to the steel access doors and activated the alarm that was beside them.

Out into the abandoned access tunnel, he turned and shut the doors, which locked securely behind him.

Sloshing through the shallow stream of water, making turns here and there, Travis slowly made his way toward the exit. He'd been down here so long; he no longer needed a map or even a flashlight. He stopped in his tracks for a moment and thought about that.

All of the things he had done and become. Through his pain and suffering he had become almost invincible. There was nothing he couldn't do. So why not stop? He didn't have to finish this. Just go away and start somewhere new. He was happy once. He could be so again.

He listened to the dripping water and then a cough suddenly escaped him. He started laughing then and the sound echoed in the tunnels as he moved on.

Finally, he arrived at the exit doors he wanted and unlocked them. These doors were almost never used, except for emergencies and the access road leading to them had long been overrun with foxtail and thistle weeds.

Nevertheless, Travis cracked open the steel door just a hair and peeked out before stepping into the clear.

Outside, Travis glanced up at the overcast sky and then crossed the road into a stand of trees.

There, he found his camouflaged pickup just as he'd left it. He removed the brush and then the canvas he had used to disguise his truck. He threw the canvas into the truck's bed and hopped behind the wheel.

He started the truck up and pulled out onto the road. The pickup bumped and bounced as it made its way down the hill and along the back roads.

Then, he came out on a small city street. A left, a right, then a couple more lefts and he headed on up to the onramp where he found himself promptly stuck in traffic.

Travis smiled to himself because he had expected something like the accident up ahead would happen. That's why he had left hours before his plan was to commence. He could walk to the downtown theater if he had to and would still be there in plenty of time to unleash his plan.

He flipped open the envelope flap and spilled the contents out onto the passenger seat. He picked up the photo of Wes Washington he had downloaded from the internet.

It had finally come to him where he knew Mr. Washington from; the Super Soldier Serum. About the same time Travis was working on the Quicksand Project, Wes had been in front of a senate intelligence committee testifying.

Wes had been the whistleblower of the Super Soldier program. Travis had been impressed and a little envious of Mr. Washington's bravado. The hearings themselves had been classified but Wes' face had been splashed across the news for weeks. Travis had wondered back then what had given Wes the courage to do what he himself could not.

Being a little worried and pursuing Wes' identity had been the right call. Wes is a smart guy, almost as smart as I am Travis thought. And if he's helping the FBI, there's a potential for them to undo the magic that Travis was performing.

"I can't have that," Travis said to himself.

He sympathized with everything Wes went through including the death of his wife but if push came to shove, Travis would show him no mercy.

Someone behind him honked their horn breaking him out of his reverie. Travis saw he had fallen behind, waved an apology and inched forward closer and closer to his next victim.

———————

"I'm not an agent. I'm a scientist," Wes said to himself as he weaved around a car. "What am I doing driving to Halli's apartment?"

The subcompact rented Ford he was driving didn't have too much power and he was honked at courtesy of the guy he almost cut off. Wes continued, alternately glancing down at the address and up at the street corner signs as he drove around the neighborhood.

He had asked for a printout of the directions at the rental place but Wes didn't notice they had given him the wrong ones until he was well on his way. He should have gotten the directions himself back at FBI headquarters but time wasn't on his side. Besides, if Brooks had caught a whiff of what Wes was up to, he might have tried to stop him.

His Ford passed 18th Street and then 19th, too. He remembered the car rental lady had mentioned it was around Farragut Square. He hung a left and then another right. Finally, he found the right street: Sunrise. He checked the address 2234 Sunrise Street, Apt. 3B.

Wes slowed the car down and cruised carefully while looking at the numbers on the homes. While looking, he saw what appeared to be a secret service agent standing next to a car talking on a cell-phone. He had been stretching and turned away from Wes. Speeding up a bit, Wes hoped that he hadn't been noticed.

Then, there on the left he saw the apartment building, Sunrise Apartments. Wes kept on driving and then made a left at the first corner he came to. He drove about halfway down the block and made a u-turn. He pulled up and parked behind a couple of cars.

From that vantage point, Wes could see the back of the apartment building above the wooden fence enclosing its perimeter. Behind the back of the apartment building were a few one story houses facing out along the rest of the street.

As Wes sat there drumming his fingers on the steering wheel trying to decide what to do next, a light rain started to come down. He peeked up through the windshield and saw a dirty, dull grey sky. He hadn't bothered to bring an umbrella or overcoat. All he had on was his sport coat. He hoped it wouldn't start snowing.

A low growl was sounded by Wes' stomach. He glanced at his watch. It read 12:30p.m.; lunchtime. After meeting Yumiko, his breakfast had consisted of coffee and stale pastries courtesy of the car rental place.

Again doubt reared its ugly head. "Why don't we just forget about this and get something to eat? The secret service is here. For all we know this Travis guy is armed. I don't even have a bulletproof vest much less a gun."

"Yeah, that's true," he answered himself. "I'm seriously allergic to lead."

Wes pulled out his cell phone and stared at it. "We could just call her and leave a message. We have her number from the printout."

"But if they traced it, Brooks would know it was you," he countered and put the phone back.

He sat but nothing else came to him. "Shit!" he

yelled and slammed his palm against the steering wheel.

Once again someone's life seemed to hang in the balance and once again, it seemed Wes wasn't up to the challenge.

Wes reached for the key in the ignition but something out of the corner of his eye caught his attention and stayed his hand.

Peering through the drizzle Wes thought he saw a black shoulder bag lying on the ground next to the Sunrise apartment fence. He was pretty sure it had been thrown over the fence. That's what had caught his eye; when it was falling. As he continued to stare at that area of the fence about half a block up, he saw first a left hand and then a right grab onto the top of the fence.

A hooded figure threw itself up and over the fence. It grabbed the bag and looked up scanning left and right, checking if its activities had been seen. The figure stood up and Wes confirmed what his mind had already guessed. "That's Halli," he whispered.

She walked to the edge of the street, checked for cars and then crossed to the other side. She angled toward a late model, silver Porsche. Wes had noted the Porsche as he had passed it coming down the block but failed to see the man inside before. Maybe he had been hunkering down.

The Porsche's driver side window came down. Halli leaned in and kissed the male occupant. She ran around the front and got in the passenger's seat.

Wes heard the motor start up and then a couple seconds later, the Porsche zipped past his rented Ford.

His stomach gurgled in protest but Wes couldn't eat now. He started the Ford and chased after Halli and the man who seemed to be her boyfriend.

They made a left and then two rights. This led their small convoy to the freeway's onramp. Why would she ditch her protection? Wes thought. Doesn't she know that she's in danger?

As they merged onto the freeway the answer occurred to Wes. No, they didn't tell her. The fools! She thinks this is just another day to play hooky from her annoying bodyguards. She has no idea the danger she's in.

Seeing as it was lunchtime, the freeway was somewhat crowded allowing Wes to follow them easily. He wondered if they were going to lunch or a motel or somewhere else. Wes also looked around at the other vehicles to see if anyone else was following them. The rain prevented him from getting a good look but as far as he could tell, there was no one else shadowing them.

Wes pulled his cell-phone out of his pocket and stared at it. Maybe I should call Yumiko. She's probably interviewing Travis' wife, though. If I call her and she comes back and it turns out it was for nothing she'll be pissed. He put the phone back and decided that he'd follow some more and call Yumiko if things got hairy.

He hoped that he wouldn't have to make that call but his instincts told him otherwise.

———

Yumiko had driven for an hour south before she finally found Carmen Cage's home. It was located in a suburban subdivision called Blue Jay Woods in northern Virginia. The house was a one story ranch style home painted a creamy yellow.

At first when Yumiko had knocked no one had

answered so she had wandered around the perimeter. She had found the ex-missus Cage in the back tending to her garden. Mrs. Cage, who reverted to her maiden name, Barragan, had been wearing headphones and didn't hear the knocking at her front door.

Ms. Barragan had been hesitant at first to answer any questions about her late husband but Yumiko could be very persuasive when she needed to be.

When people saw Yumiko's friendly and delicate Japanese features, they opened up to her pretty quickly. They usually didn't know that at five-foot nine, 150 pounds, and with a black-belt in Taekwondo, Yumiko could be persuasive by force too, if necessary.

As is was, Yumiko didn't go into details, but when Ms. Barragan realized that young girls' lives were somehow at stake her resolve against invasions into her privacy broke down. She agreed to help in any way that she could.

"So, you're saying that something I know about my ex-husband might be useful to you?" Carmen Barragan asked.

Yumiko shifted in her seat and set the tea cup she had been holding down. "That's right, Ms. Barragan. People sometimes know information that may be helpful without even realizing it."

Carmen took a sip of her earl grey tea before answering and set it back down on its saucer. "I've thrown out everything of my ex's. I had a really difficult time there at the end of our relationship. Also, he kept his work pretty much a secret. I knew very little about it."

"Well, just relax and take your time. I'll ask some questions and if you feel uncomfortable just tell me and we'll move on. Okay?"

After hesitating for a moment, Carmen nodded her assent.

"Let's start with the divorce itself. Why did it happen?" Yumiko asked.

"Looking back on it all now, it was easy to blame Travis. Even after all of the devastating things that happened to us, if he would have just walked away, I would've forgiven him anything. But he just couldn't let it go.

"After Travis got his PhD, he went to work for a small company doing cancer research. We had Isabella and our life was beautiful," Carmen sighed.

"This is Isabella?" Yumiko asked pointing to a framed photo on the coffee table.

"Was, yes. That was part of the tragedy that destroyed our marriage. Soon after the first Gulf War ended, Travis was recruited to work for military intelligence. And at first everything was still wonderful."

Military intel? Eric King? Yumiko thought.

"Go on," Yumiko prodded.

"But in the summer of 2003 everything changed. I remember it clearly because it was somehow related to those hearings on TV about the soldier experiments. Travis was often coming home late. He was usually stressed out from pressure at work. When he would see what little they showed of the classified hearings on the news, he would practically explode."

"Did you ever find out why?"

"No, I never did but it had something to do with the war. But what didn't back then?"

Yumiko smiled and reached for a tea cake from the tray Carmen had set out.

Carmen continued after another sip of her tea.

"Then when our daughter became sick his rages turned into paranoia and depression. Sometimes late at night when he thought I was asleep, I would hear him weeping in our bathroom. Between the sobs, he'd be saying, 'It's my fault', over and over again."

"What do you think he meant by that?"

"I can't imagine. The doctors all said Isabella had a rare form of bone cancer. They said there was no way anyone could have seen it coming or prevented it, even if they had. It couldn't have been his fault. I tried to make him listen but we were hardly speaking at that point.

"Isabella died on December 15th of that year. That was hard and then early the next year Travis' mom died. She lived on a small farm by herself over in Frederick County. The medical examiner indicated that she died of natural causes in her sleep but Travis went nuts. He went into this whole intricate conspiracy theory about how someone was out to destroy him. I didn't understand any of it."

At the mention of bone cancer, Yumiko had left her tea to grow cold. Instead she had pulled out her PDA and was busy pecking notes into it. She asked, "Did he ever tell you specifically, who, was out to get him?"

Carmen wrung her hands and stared out at her patio where raindrops could be seen falling to the ground. "One night a few weeks before he died, he had gotten really drunk. He tried to tell me who he imagined was doing all this to him but at the last minute he backed off. He said that if he told me, they'd get me, too.

"I never saw him again after that night. The papers said he died partly because we were getting a divorce but I don't think he ever even saw the divorce papers. I filed them and left them on the table for him, but I think he had decided to kill himself long before that. Maybe in his own way he was trying to protect me."

At that point, Carmen broke down crying. She tried to stifle the wracking sobs that caused her chest to heave violently.

Yumiko went to her, hugged her and said, "It's okay, Carmen. Let it out. Just let it all out."

After awhile of sitting on the couch holding Yumiko while she cried, Carmen excused herself. She went into the bathroom to freshen up. Yumiko returned to her seat and took the opportunity to review her notes. She wanted to make sure she hadn't missed anything. She'd need all the ammunition she could muster when she appealed for her badge back.

"Sorry I kept you waiting," Carmen said when she returned. She sat down again across from Yumiko.

"No problem," Yumiko said, "I just have a couple more questions and then I'll be on my way. You're really helping me a lot here and I appreciate it."

"Sure," Carmen responded with a sad smile. "You know, this has actually felt good getting it all out in the open. I feel as if a heavy weight's been lifted off my chest. I've kept it all bottled up for so long."

Yumiko nodded her sympathy and said, "You mentioned Travis' mother. I'm sorry, what was her name?"

"Margaret. Her name was Margaret Cage and before that, I believe it was Anderson."

"Yes, Margaret. Whatever happened to her land or the farmhouse?"

Carmen scratched her head for a moment and then smoothed it with her hand. She said, "You know, now that you mention it, I guess since Travis never signed those papers it's mine. None of his relatives ever stepped forward to claim it. But I haven't been out there in years. It's probably just like it was when Margaret died, unless someone's stolen something. My goodness, I guess I should find out. What do you think?"

Yumiko thought about it for a split second before answering. "Well, why don't you let me take a look out there first? Make sure there's nothing dangerous. I'll let you know when it's safe."

Carmen hesitated but then said, "Okay, if you think that's best."

"Yes, I absolutely think that would be best," Yumiko affirmed.

Travis checked the two syringes one last time. He made sure the pressurized injection systems were in working order and then put them back in his pockets.

The guy sitting in the stall next to him grunted a couple more times and then Travis could hear wiping. The guy stood, pulled up his pants and fastened his belt as the toilet flushed automatically from the motion sensors.

The guy opened the door and stepped out of the stall. Instead of hearing running water, Travis heard the bathroom exit door open and then shut a few seconds later. He briefly heard the sounds of the theater patrons out in the lobby.

People didn't bother washing their hands these days. They were so afraid of catching something from the faucet that they didn't even touch it. It didn't occur to them that *they* might have something and be passing it around by not washing. If Travis had had an extra syringe he would've followed that guy and given him something to really worry about.

As it was, he didn't have the extra syringe or the time to teach such a disgusting person a lesson. According to Halli's conversation with her boyfriend, they were supposed to be at the theater to see the 1:30 p.m. showing of Twilight Dance.

Travis had puzzled for a long time over how to get past those Secret Service agents and his target had solved the problem for him. Travis was sure that his mission was divine. Even if the Secret Service was tailing her, Travis felt he'd still succeed today.

He remembered a line from a detective movie he once saw; 'The best way to follow someone was to get there before them' or something to that effect. That guy couldn't have been more right. Travis checked his ticket; Twilight Dance theater number 2. He checked his watch; 1:15, time to go.

Once off the freeway, Wes had lost the Porsche. "Fuck!" he yelled and beat his fist against the steering wheel.

The rain had started in earnest as the Porsche zipped in, out and between the other cars; something Wes couldn't do without giving himself away or risking an accident. The last he saw of the Porsche was when it zipped through an intersection a few cars up ahead just as the light turned red. By the time the light had changed to green and Wes went through the intersection, the Porsche was long gone.

Wes was on the main boulevard though and figured they had stopped somewhere along it. He moved to the far right lane, slowed and scanned the parking lots for the Porsche.

After a few minutes of this, though, the car behind him honked and Wes could hear a faint shout. Wes pulled into the first turn-in he came to. He found himself in a shopping center; a grocery store was the anchor with small shops on either side.

He began to drive up and down the parking lot looking for the Porsche. Wes supposed that it was the only way he'd be able to find them. Even though it was like looking for a needle in a haystack, what other choice did he have? Wes just hoped nothing happened to them in the meantime.

———————

The theater seated about four hundred people from what Travis could tell. He was sitting in the aisle seat on the right side near the entrance. His shoes were semi-glued to the sticky spilled soda under his feet. And what was that smell? He wondered.

When Halli and her boyfriend, Kurt came in, he spotted them immediately. Actually, he had spotted Kurt first as his six-foot-two muscular frame was hard to miss. Kurt had played some college football and retained a lot of his bulk, even though the only things he was hitting these days were law books.

The lights started to dim as Halli and Kurt took their seats. They were sitting in the center a few rows up from the back. A thirty-something couple was sitting directly behind them. Travis had anticipated this though and moved quickly to sit next to the thirty-something couple as the first preview started. Travis coughed a dry hacking cough a couple of times and wiped his mouth. The couple looked over at the elderly black man. He touched the woman's hand with his spittle covered one and said, "I'm sorry, I didn't cough on you did I?"

"No, it's okay," said the woman as she looked at Travis with sympathy.

They weren't getting the hint so Travis managed to 'accidentally' step on the woman's leather boot. Her husband noticed and whispered, "Let's move."

His wife protested by saying, "He's just a harmless old man."

"I don't care," replied her husband, "let's just move."

The wife acquiesced and the couple moved a few rows up. Travis took the seat directly behind Halli.

The best opening to infect Halli was a fifty-fifty shot Travis summed up. On the one hand he could just go for her neck but if she moved or twisted her neck, he might miss. On the other hand, Halli was leaning in toward her boyfriend which exposed her side and back through the seat slit. Travis put his hand up to the slit and visually measured the width of the gap. He decided that he could in fact slip his hand through with no problem.

The previews had ended and the main feature had started. The dim lights went out and the theater was cst into darkness.

Travis scanned the theater. There were only about twenty or thirty people scattered about; couples mostly. They all seemed to be settling comfortably into watching the movie. No time like the present, he thought and slowly pulled out the syringe from his right pocket.

Just as Travis was preparing to strike, Wes spotted the silver Porsche in the theater's parking lot outside. He pulled up next to it and jumped out of his rental.

The rain was coming down pretty heavy so he

pulled up the collar on his sport coat and dashed toward the box office.

When he got to the box office he realized that he had no clue as to which show they were watching. Wes scanned the tickertape movie titles as they moved from left to right. He checked his watch. It read 1:45 p.m. Glancing back up at the tickertape, Wes confirmed that there were three movies that had started around that time. But why did he feel an irresistible urge to screw getting the ticket and rush inside? He found the Porsche; he could just wait for them to come out, couldn't he?

A reasonable argument, but Wes knew why he shouldn't wait. If he was the killer, a dark crowded movie theater would be the perfect place to strike. As Yumiko had said often enough, 'That's what I would do if I were him'.

Wes' indecision was really starting to spook him. He could feel the hair standing up on the back of his neck. Then, Wes heard what he could have sworn was a scream. Maybe it was just the wind his mind protested. But as he peered into the theater, he could clearly see two ushers running across the lobby and into the back part of the theater.

Although Kurt was much bigger than the strange old man and could probably take him easy, Halli had seen the cold insanity in the man's eyes. She had screamed as much to draw help as to express her fear.

Kurt held the man's right arm up in the air with his left hand. Travis cursed himself. He had missed with his first lunge at Halli. She had pulled back at the last possible moment and seen his syringe sticking through the seat gap. Kurt being quick for a big guy had grabbed Travis' arm with an iron grip and was trying to twist the syringe out of his hand.

Of course, Travis was always prepared. He slipped the fingers of his left hand under his belt and withdrew the scalpel he kept hidden there.

The scalpel glinted and flashed in the projector's light. The scalpel's large shadow was cast on the screen. Some in the audience yelled for Travis and Kurt to sit down and shut-up. But the ones who were close enough to see the surgical knife smartly headed for the back exits; quickly.

Kurt roared in pain as the scalpel slashed deep into his wrist slicing the tendon. He instantly let go of Travis' arm as his hand became useless. Warm sticky blood seeped through Kurt's fingers as he used his right hand to try to staunch the flow. He yelled at Halli, "Run! Get out of here now, Halli!"

Halli hesitated. She didn't want to leave Kurt.

"I said, run, goddammit!" Kurt yelled at her.

Halli took off running down the aisle toward the exit at the front of the theater, next to the screen.

Travis stabbed Kurt in the abdomen. Kurt buckled. Travis paused long enough to wag his finger in a 'no, no' gesture at Kurt before chasing after Halli. Kurt made a last ditch grab at Travis but slipped and fell between the seats and onto the dirty floor.

When the ushers had run into the back of the theater, Wes guessed that if Travis was in there, he'd be leaving out the front. Wes made his way around and to the rear of the theater complex.

Halli burst through the exit door and into the back alley behind the theater. The fat raindrops obscured her vision at first, so she couldn't make out which way was her path to safety. She heard footsteps coming up the stairs behind her. She turned and ran down the alley to the left.

After about ten yards, she saw two large metal

trash bins in front of a high wall. There were two halogen lamps high on the wall shining on the bins.

Halli jumped on top of the bin on the left in an effort to get over the wall. Unfortunately, the wall was not only too high for her to reach, but she could see it was topped with barbed wire as well. She turned to run back the other way but stopped in her tracks when she saw the old man standing there.

"What do you want from me?" Halli screamed at the man.

The old man cocked his head to the right as if listening for something but didn't answer her.

Wes had seen what appeared to be an old man walking down the alley a few yards in front of him. After the clown performance, he assumed correctly that the old man was Travis in disguise. He had him. If only he could get close enough and get the drop on him. He passed the still open exit door and continued following as quietly as possible.

Halli saw an African-American man in a drenched sport coat moving up slowly behind the old man. He was still several feet behind the old man. This second man put a finger up to his lips and then made a stretching gesture with his hands. Halli got it: don't say anything about me and stall.

"I don't know you. I've never done anything to you. Why are you trying to hurt me?" Halli pleaded from the top of the trash bin.

The old man still said nothing. He took a couple of steps closer to Halli and stopped. He cocked his head to the left and stared at her.

Just then, Kurt came lumbering down the alley. He was blinded by the rain and pain but thought he saw the old man crouched in front of him. With the last of what energy he could muster, he roared and brought his arm down like a club on top of the old man's head.

Halli shouted, "No, Kurt, don't!" as Kurt dropped the hammer on the man in the sport coat.

Wes looked up just in time to see Kurt's arm come down on his head. Pain exploded into his skull and he dropped to the ground.

His life spent, Kurt collapsed on top of Wes.

In all the confusion, Halli had lost track of the old man. She realized where he had gone when she felt the sting and pressure in her thigh. She looked down to see the old man grinning up at her. She kicked at the old man but he avoided it easily.

Whatever he had injected her with must have contained some sort of sedative as Halli immediately began to feel drowsy. She slid down and off of the trash bin. She tried to fight the effects of the sedative and crawl to Kurt just a few feet away. She only managed a few inches before she succumbed to the drug and passed out.

Wes slowly rolled Kurt off of himself and tried to sit up, but pain exploded in his temple driving him back to the ground. From his prone position he reached out to check Kurt's vitals. With the rain, blood and his pounding skull, he couldn't be positive, but he was pretty sure Kurt was dead.

Remembering why he had come down the ally in the first place, Wes looked around for Travis. He was rewarded for his effort with a kick to his side which doubled him over once more. He could feel hands flipping him over.

"Wes Washington," Travis said. "Sorry, it had to be like this. I'm sure you're just a pawn in all this, like I was."

The doubled image of Travis' face swimmed above Wes' as he croaked, "Cage..."

"Ah," Travis said, "so you and the feds have

figured out who I really am. Too bad, I liked being old Harold. But did they tell you why I'm doing this, Wes? Ask them why they wouldn't help my little girl when you see them. Tell Cole, that it's her own fault. And tell Brooks that I'm doing Serena a favor."

Travis pulled out his back-up syringe, leaned down and injected it into Wes' neck. Wes screamed at the pain.

Voices at the far end of the alley could be heard.

"Sounds like our time is up," Travis said. "To tell you the truth, I don't know what that's going to do to you. If there's a reaction, maybe they'll help you. They wouldn't help my daughter, but maybe they'll help you. Either way, that's the only warning you get. Next time you're dead. Ta-ta, Wes."

Travis stood and then waved before running out of the alley.

Wes tried to stand and give chase. He made it to a bent over standing position but the first step reduced him to tears and he fell back to the ground. He lay on the ground staring up at the grey sky as the rain pelted his face.

———

Wes leaned up against the ambulance with an ice pack pressed to the back of his head.

He was angry but he told himself he had to let all that go. Still, he couldn't believe that the police had tried to arrest him.

When he woke up in the ambulance, he had found himself cuffed to the stretcher. The police office standing guard had begun reading Wes his rights when he saw that Wes had gained consciousness.

Wes proclaimed his innocence but the police

weren't having any of it. So, Wes ended up placing a call to Yumiko after all. After speaking to Yumiko on Wes' cell-phone, the cops had uncuffed Wes and apologized.

Then the paramedics had wanted to take Wes into the hospital for overnight observation as he had a mild concussion and bruised ribs. Wes resisted and the paramedics dropped it, but they did insist that he wait for a ride. They weren't about to let him drive anywhere. He told them that Yumiko was coming for him so they let him up and out of the ambulance. That had been about twenty minutes ago.

Yumiko hadn't been happy with Wes when she got his call but didn't argue on the phone. He supposed she was saving her tirade to do it in person.

He glanced over at the crime scene. Yellow tape cordoned off the back of the theater. Police, federal agents and crime scene personnel wandered back and forth. Wes couldn't see what they were doing but he knew they hadn't taken Kurt's body away, yet.

Kurt's parents had somehow got wind of the location of their son's body and had come to the scene. Kurt's father had demanded to see his son but the police had refused. Kurt's mother had burst into tears. A police detective had convinced them to accompany him to the police station and they had gone.

Wes had looked for Halli when he woke up in the ambulance but apparently her father's security detail had shown up and spirited her away.

Brooks hadn't shown up. Wes had prepared his lie that he had been out getting some lunch when he spotted Travis. But Brooks never came and the new FBI team had simply told Wes to come in to the Annex tomorrow. They'd interview him then.

Something was seriously wrong with this investigation.

A honk sounded a few yards away from Wes. He turned his head and saw Yumiko with her arm sticking out the window, waving him over.

"My ride's here," Wes said to the paramedic standing near him and pointed at Yumiko's sedan.

"All right. I wish you'd go in for observation, but remember what I told you. If you vomit, feel nauseous, sleepy or an increase in head pain, then come in immediately," the paramedic cautioned.

"Will do," Wes said. He tossed the ice pack into a nearby trashcan as he walked to Yumiko's car.

He got in, shut the door and fastened his seatbelt.

"Hey," Wes said and smiled at Yumiko.

"Hey!" Yumiko yelled as she pulled away from the theater. "Is that all you have to say to me? What... the fuck... did I tell you, Wes?"

"You told me not to do anything stupid," Wes confessed.

"If you didn't already have that bump on your head, I'd give you one myself," she shouted.

"I'm sorry," Wes said. And he really was. Yumiko could see the anguish on his face.

"All, right. I'm not mad at you. Much. You just really scared the shit out of me when you called. You sounded like death warmed over. Maybe it's good that you got that bump on your noggin. Something to remind you next time you get the urge to play cop," Yumiko scolded.

A loud growl erupted from Wes' stomach.

Yumiko glanced at the clock on the dash. It read: 5:05p.m. "Have you eaten anything since breakfast?" she asked.

"Actually, no, in all the excitement with my

adrenalin pumping, I completely forget about eating," he answered.

"Okay," Yumiko said, "there's a little diner up here on the corner. We'll get you something and we can compare the day's notes."

Wes nodded his agreement, especially to the part about getting something in his empty belly.

Just before the corner, they pulled into the parking lot. The neon sign on the small diner said: Marty's. Simple and to the point Wes thought as Yumiko parked right in front in the space nearest the door. They got out and headed in.

The grey sky still threatened rain but Wes figured the downpour was over for now, in more ways than one.

A sign reading, 'Please Wait to be Seated,' greeted them in the foyer, so they did.

A few moments later, a young pony-tailed woman came up and guided them to a booth toward the back.

The server introduced herself as Meadow and handed them menus. They settled into the well-worn, red leather seats as Meadow asked, "Would either of you like something to drink to start you off?"

"Coffee. Black." Yumiko replied.

"And I'll have a glass of orange juice," Wes said.

Meadow walked off to give them time to peruse the menu.

Wes smelled gravy and his stomach growled loudly again.

"So, fill me in on the details," Yumiko said.

As Wes worked his way through the food and drink that Meadow brought periodically, he related his tale.

He conveniently omitted the part about being

infected. No need to bring that up without first running some tests on himself, Wes thought. Yumiko pushed the apple pie she had ordered around on her plate and didn't interrupt as Wes proceeded.

When he was done with his entrée and talking, he ordered dessert and wolfed that down as Yumiko told him about her interview with Ms. Barragan.

When she was done awhile later, Wes said, "So, let's see what we've got. He's infected four of his main targets out of a probable five."

"And he's close enough to the end that he really doesn't care to come out in the open or if we know who he is," Yumiko added.

"Do you think you can catch him at this farmhouse?" Wes asked.

"Well, he's got to go underground for a time anyway just to see what our next move is before he makes his. So there's a chance. But now tell me again, what did he tell you about his daughter?"

Wes attempted to scratch his head but the bump reminded him with a jolt of pain that that was a no-no. He folded his hands on the table instead and said, "Well, basically Travis said to ask you guys about his daughter. He said you, meaning the government, feds, etc., wouldn't save her."

"Not 'couldn't' but 'wouldn't'?" Yumiko clarified.

"Well, my head was pounding at the time but yeah, I'm pretty sure it was 'wouldn't'," Wes said.

"I think you were right, Wes," Yumiko said shaking her head. "There's something deeper going on here."

Meadow came by and dropped off the check. "Can I get you guys anything else?"

Yumiko and Wes both declined.

"Okay, then you guys have a nice night," Meadow said with a smile before walking away.

Yumiko took the check and looked at it. Wes reached for his wallet and his cell-phone rang.

He pulled it out and flipped it open. "Hello."

Yumiko, not hearing anything looked up from the check to Wes' face. Silent tears were spilling down both his cheeks.

All Wes could muster was a weak, "No..." before he ended the call.

Yumiko could imagine what had happened but Wes said it anyway, "Alex is dead."

Tuesday — December 7

"Almost there," Travis said to the small photo of his daughter, Isabella. He put the dog-eared photo back into his wallet and left it on the coffee table.

He got up from the sofa and walked into his laboratory. He glanced at the clock at the bottom of one of the computer screens. It read: 6:00 AM. Travis had taken a nap as soon as he got back from dealing with Halli. Since he had woken up at midnight, he had been doing final preparations on his next and last target.

In the clean room, the suspension for Serena's injection was being generated.

He called up a program on his computer with a few clicks of the mouse. On his screen was a map of Washington, D.C. A flashing red blip could be seen clearly in the downtown area. Travis tapped the screen and said, "Morning, Serena."

Almost a year ago Travis had briefly broken into Director Brooks' home when he and his family were abroad. It was very risky but necessary. He had planted several tracking devices on clothes items and accessories he had previously observed Serena wearing. Oh, yes, he knew exactly where she was.

The software and satellite tracking device he was

using was for military personnel only. Travis had acquired it from an Army supply Sergeant who had an addiction to heroin. No way, he could have said no, to the cash Travis had laid on him for the equipment. Especially, when Travis had misrepresented himself as a covert agent. Working for the military for so long had taught him more than a few tricks.

With another few clicks of the mouse, Travis shut down the program. Based on the position of the blip, he knew where she was. The formula wouldn't be ready anyway for another eight hours, so Travis could use the time to obtain some last items he'd need to finish up his masterpiece. He had already decided on the appropriate disguise, but he'd need the proper identification to go with it.

He turned and headed back into his living area.

From his refrigerator he pulled out a bottle of apple juice and sipped it. He picked up the remote in his off-hand and turned on the television.

As he drank, he flipped through the channels looking for any news of last night's exploits. He couldn't find any and assumed that Brooks had a news blackout in effect, at least temporarily. He wondered how long Brooks could maintain it.

"Oh well, it doesn't matter," Travis said out loud. "After your sweet Serena is infected, you'll be screaming to the world for help, you bastard, Brooks."

Yumiko had to park across the street and down a ways from Senator Cole's home as the driveway was already crowded with cars.

Wes and Yumiko got out and crossed the street,

headed toward the driveway.

A young disheveled young man who had been lurking behind some bushes intercepted them on the sidewalk. He shoved a digital recorder under their noses and said, "Rick North, Independent Press. Do you have any comment on the death of Alexandra Cole?"

Wes just shook his head. Yumiko strong armed the recorder out of her face and said, "No comment."

"The press won't be denied. I know there's something going on here. The truth will come out eventually and you'll be on record as lying about not knowing," the frustrated reporter yelled out as they walked on.

It seemed as though the mainstream media still hadn't caught on but an independent journalist was doing his job. He stalked them, peppering them with questions. "Hey wait, I know you sir, don't I? Yes, I'm sure I know you from somewhere. Are you a part of this investigation?"

Yumiko and Wes ignored him and when they got onto the Cole estate proper the reporter gave up the chase. He retreated back to the bushes to lay in wait for the next visitor. He probably didn't want to stay near the driveway thanks to the big, burly guard at the front door.

The guard had Yumiko and Wes show him some identification. Then they waited for a few minutes as he notified someone inside the house as to their presence on his walkie-talkie.

A young woman came out of the front door and said, "Hi, my name's Tamara. I'm Janet's niece. She said to come on in. She's out in the back."

Wes and Yumiko made their way through the foyer and down the hall toward the kitchen. Wes glanced at the chair he had fallen asleep in just a few days before. A child sat in it now playing a hand-held video game.

Friends and family members milled about, talking in hushed tones. Children were running back and forth in the living room. Wes saw a couple kids run up the stairs and he wondered if the airlock was still in place up there. Probably not.

"Hey Greg," Wes said to Senator Cole's husband as they entered the kitchen. "How are you holding up?"

"Best as I can under the circumstances," he said. "There's plenty of food and drink if you want, so help yourselves."

Wes noted the filled shot glass in Greg's hand and the pint of whiskey next to it. Wes couldn't blame him, though. He himself had gotten to know Jack Daniels intimately after the death of Chiang-Mei.

"Janet's out in the garden," Greg said before downing his current shot and reaching for the bottle. "She's out there with that asshole, Brooks."

Good, thought Yumiko, 'cause it's finally time for some answers.

Wes and Yumiko stepped out onto the patio and looked for Cole and Brooks. They were in the west corner of the garden sitting on a pair of long stone benches. Wes and Yumiko made a beeline for Cole and Brooks.

Janet saw them and rose to greet them. Her eyes were red and a little puffy from crying but she seemed to be holding up okay now. "Thank you for coming," she said and grasped Wes' and Yumiko's hands.

"Sorry, for your loss, ma'am," Yumiko said.

Brooks had stayed seated and hadn't bothered to acknowledge them, which was fine by Wes.

"I don't think...," Wes said and then paused. "What I mean to say is, you asked me to help and..."

"It's okay, Wes, you did what you could. I know that," Janet said as she gave Wes' hand a squeeze.

Yumiko glanced at Wes and he noted the subtlest of nods. He and Yumiko had gone over their game plan in the morning before coming to the Senator's home. It was perhaps cruel but it was the only way they felt they could get at the truth. That nod was Wes' signal to begin.

"Thanks, I appreciate that. Did you hear about yesterday by the way?" Wes asked holding Janet's gaze.

"About you getting attacked by that animal?" Janet asked. "Yes, Karl filled me in just before you came."

"Did Karl tell you that an innocent young man died, too?" Yumiko asked.

Janet glanced at Brooks and then said, "Well, yes, Karl mentioned something but what are you getting at here. What do you mean innocent? Are you implying that the other victims are somehow not innocent?"

"When I was laying there on the ground, this maniac Travis, asked me to ask you guys something," Wes said turning his gaze on Brooks and then back to Cole. "Do you know what it was?"

Janet hesitated and turned to Brooks for support, "I..."

Brooks stood then and pulled the senator back from Wes and Yumiko. He said, "Don't answer that. I thought I told you to stick to the lab, Mr. Washington. And you're suspended, Yamazaki. You have no right to be asking questions. If you're done giving your condolences, then you can go."

"He wanted to know why you wouldn't help his

little girl," Wes said looking at the senator hard. "And he said it's your own fault."

Slowly, tears began to well up in the senator's eyes.

"Goddammit!" Brooks yelled. "Hasn't she suffered enough? Now you're conveying the sentiments of a serial killer to a grieving mother. Whose side are you on, Wes?"

"No, whose side are *you* on?" Yumiko asked Brooks as she pointed a finger at him. "From the beginning you've tried to sidetrack us and slow us down in this investigation.

"I've talked to Travis' ex-wife. This guy was into some deep shit and a lot of pressure came down from up on high to destroy him. He knew what was coming and faked his own death to get out from under it. And now he's getting his revenge. Girl by girl. And yeah, Brooks, your daughter is next on the list. Tell me again that you don't know anything about this."

Brooks' face turned scarlet red. He stepped closer to Yumiko in a menacing way, but quickly saw she wasn't intimidated. "Look, you have no right..."

Through her tears, Janet screamed, "Shut-up! All of you just shut-up!"

Although Wes and Yumiko had hoped she'd crack, they were still stunned by her rage and looked at her in amazement.

"Okay, if you want to know, I'll tell you. I've lost my daughter but you won't be satisfied until I lose it all, will you?" Janet yelled.

"Think about the presidency," Brooks advised. "And besides, I don't think you have clearance..."

"Karl, shut... the fuck... up... and sit your ass down," Janet commanded.

As instructed Karl sat down on the stone bench.

Wes thought that Janet Cole could indeed have made a good president. Her inner strength was impressive.

Janet wiped at her tears and gathered herself. She turned to Wes and Yumiko and leveled a steely gaze at them. She said, "Travis is right, it is my own fault. From the moment they told me Alex's illness wasn't natural, I knew Travis Cage was behind it. I couldn't save Alex for the exact same reason he couldn't save Isabella; our orders prevented it. That's why I had you brought in Wes. I thought that if there was anyone who was smart enough to beat Travis at his sick game, without forcing me to breach national security, it was you. But I guess I was wrong."

I knew it. Like always, I just knew it, Wes thought. He glanced over at Yumiko who was shaking her head at Brooks.

Brooks gave her the finger like a petulant teenager but remained quiet as Janet had commanded.

Yumiko turned to Cole and said, "Take it from the top, Senator, and don't leave anything out. We couldn't save Alex, but there's still time to save the other girls."

Senator Cole waved a dismissive hand at Yumiko. "I know. I know. I'll tell you everything."

———————

I was walking to my car late one evening in the fall of 2002. This was after the Super Soldier hearings were finished.

I had my car keys out and had just reached my vehicle. I was about to unlock the door when a voice out of the shadows whispered, "Senator Cole?"

I whipped my head around to see where the

sound had come from, but I saw no one. I held my keys firmly in my hand, ready to strike if attacked. The voice said, "Don't be alarmed. I mean you no harm. In fact, I need your help."

"Who's there?" I asked.

A man stepped out from behind a pillar ten feet away and said, "Cage. My name's Travis Cage and I pray to god that you can help me."

I had never heard of or seen him before. He looked a bit disheveled and had dark circles under his eyes, but he didn't appear dangerous. I loosened my grip on my keys a little and asked, "Who are you? What do you want?"

"I'm a scientist with military intelligence. I'm working on something that needs to be stopped, but I can't do it alone. I saw how you handled the whole Super Soldier thing and I need that kind of help, too," Travis said as he took a step closer.

"What are you working on?" I asked him.

Just then, footsteps could be heard drawing near. Two women were walking toward their cars. Travis didn't answer and slid back into the shadows behind the pillar.

The two women said their goodbyes, got into their cars and drove off. Travis reappeared and said, "It would be best if we didn't talk here; too many ears and eyes. Can we meet somewhere?"

"There's a mom and pop cafe a couple of blocks up on the right. Do you know where I'm talking about?" I asked.

He nodded and said, "I'll meet you there in ten minutes." He then disappeared back among the cars.

I got into my car but didn't leave right away. Sitting there with my keys in my lap, I considered all that I'd gone through with the Super Soldier hearings. It had drained me. But it was my duty, too.

I started the car and drove to the meeting point.

When I entered the coffee shop, Travis was already seated in the back. He had his back to a windowless corner of the open, spacious room. He had positioned his chair to more easily monitor who was coming into and out of the place. There was a mug sitting on the small round table in front of him. As I drew close, I could see his eyes ping-ponging from the entrance, to the exit in the back, and back to the entrance again.

I sat across from him and asked, "Do you think someone's following you?"

He shrugged. "Sometimes I'm pretty sure someone is. Other times... I'm not so sure. I suppose that's part of their plan, too. Make me doubt my own reality."

"Who's plan?" I asked. I'd only just met him but I was starting to fear for his mental state.

He shrugged again. "CIA, Military Intel. They're all the same really. Pots and kettles. Kettles and pots."

The restroom door in the back near us, slammed against the wall and a kid came bouncing out. Travis nearly jumped out of his shoes at the sound.

With a shaky hand, he took a sip from his mug. It smelled like hot chocolate. He noticed me watching and said, "Sorry, where are my manners? Would you like something?"

"I'll get it myself, thanks," I said. I got up and went to the counter. I ordered some coffee and paid. When it was ready, I took it back to our table and sat back down. By then, Travis seemed a bit more calm. Guess what they say about chocolate having calming properties is true.

"Sorry, I seem to keep jumping from topic to topic. Let me start from the beginning," he said.

"Okay," I said and took off my coat. I laid it on the back of the empty chair next to me.

"Like I said, I work for military intelligence. To put it simply, I've been working on a top secret weapon to kill the terrorists."

"What?" I almost yelled.

Travis looked around to make sure no one had noticed my outburst and then bent in closer. He whispered, "Remember how the U.S. government used small pox in the blankets they gave to the Native Americans to wipe them out? Well, imagine if instead of blankets, the victims themselves were also the carriers. Imagine if you had a person's DNA and you could use that to mark the person or persons. Then, you could use that marker to infect that target with any disease you wanted. If a few people died of the flu and then a few more and then, before you know it a whole race of people, who would be the wiser?"

"No, they wouldn't!" I protested.

"They would and they have," Travis said and laughed bitterly. "The project is codenamed 'Quicksand'. We're really quite close. We've already done it with animals; rats, pigs, horses, apes. Now we've started with human trials; the homeless, military prisoners."

"But who would consent to do something like this?" I asked shaken.

"To tell you the truth, when I started on the project, I didn't know what they had us working on. I thought it was a cure for our women and men out in the field. But as I moved up and became the project's lead researcher they had to tell me what it was really about. They laid so much patriotic guilt on me though, that I didn't even blink twice. I kept right on plugging away."

"So what are you doing here? What changed your mind?" I asked.

"Crossover," he replied holding my gaze with his own.

"Sorry, I learned a lot during the Super Soldier briefings, but I'm still no expert in biology. What does crossover mean?"

"It's basically the way genetic information is exchanged. More specifically, we were using this technique in our original mice subjects to introduce the marker into their genetic structure.

"Anyway, to make a long story short, even as we advanced to human trials, one of our young, bright researchers kept on working with the mice. She found that in a third generation of mice, our marked gene turned up. In the fourth generation there was crossover and 99% percent of those mice died."

I thought I understood what he had said, but asked him anyway. "So what you're saying is that if a particular race were targeted that a few generations later the whole human race could possibly die?"

Travis nodded grimly. "Now you've got it. If we target Arab Target A and the marker gets away, the whole family of Arab Target A could die. Then, whole Arab populations, then the Middle-east, then..."

"...the world," I finished for him.

Travis lifted his cup to his lips for another sip but found it empty. He shrugged at his mistake, put the cup back down and said, "We thought we were so clever."

We both sat silent for a moment, listening to the wind howl outside. Then I asked, "Did you try to warn them? The Pentagon? The Secretary of Defense? I mean, I'm sure you had data proving what would happen."

"Oh, yes, we tried to warn them. We took our

evidence to the head of the project, Dr. Roland
Wilhelm first. He said he would handle it but weeks
and then months went by with no word. So, I
personally went over his head. I appealed as high up
the chain of command I could go.

"But our warnings were dismissed every step of
the way. You know, 'National Security' and the
'Global War on Terror' all took precedence. The
woman who had discovered the crossover was
transferred out and threatened with prison time if
she squawked. Treason and all that. They tried
threatening me, too, until I hinted that I'd quit and
take copies of my work to the press. As their lead
researcher, I told them, two things would happen if I
did that. One, their project would be dead in the
water. And two, everyone would believe me."

"How did they respond to that?"

Travis laughed. "They backed-off and said they'd
suspend the project immediately while they
investigated my claims. And me like an idiot, I
believed them."

"So, they lied?" I asked, having heard many
similar stories before.

"Of course they lied," Travis said, "but they even
did me one better. Two weeks after supposedly
shutting the project down, they brought me in for
what was supposed to be my debriefing. They
debriefed me all right.

"They showed me the pictures of how they had
infected my daughter, Isabella, with the marker.
They said they didn't know what it would do to her
seeing as how it was designed for a Middle-
Easterner, but they were sure it wouldn't be good."

"Oh, my gosh!" escaped my lips. I glanced
around and confirmed that there was no one within
earshot of Travis' declaration.

"They had me of course. I was so angry at first that I wanted to bring a pistol into the Pentagon and gun them all down. But how would that save my daughter?"

"It wouldn't."

"Exactly, so I jumped back into the lab as fast as I could. That's when I found out that the operation had been moved to another location just to fool me. Nothing had stopped. Everything was running full speed ahead. I had to perfect the marker and find the cure for it, all at the same time. I've been working night and day with no sleep for weeks, but I'm no closer to a cure than when I first started. My wife thinks I'm mad and I can tell her nothing, lest I put her in harm's way, too. Maybe I am mad."

"And your daughter?"

"Although she's shown no overt symptoms of sickness, she's been getting weaker and weaker day by day. She's exhibiting something akin to fibromyalgia. System wide aches, pains and illness. She's a tough little one, but I don't know how long she can hold out."

"What can I do?" I asked.

Travis' dark eyes grew a bit brighter and hopeful at my offer to help. He said, "I need you to help me expose this dangerous weapon to the world. Then, I can get some people a whole lot smarter than me to help me save my daughter. The international community is way ahead of us on this stuff; cloning, stem cell research, and so on. I don't care if they get me for treason or whatever after. Hell, I'll put the death penalty needle in myself, but I must save my daughter."

"How old is she?" I asked thinking about my own daughter, Alex.

"She's twelve," he said.

All I could do was nod. I knew exactly how he felt. My daughter was twelve, too, at that time. And, like him, I would've done anything to protect her.

"Okay," I said. "I'm on relatively good terms with the Secretary of Defense, Frank Alfaro. I'll see what I can find out."

I could practically feel his relief from the look on his face. He reached out with both of his shaking hands and grasped mine within his. "Oh, thank you. Thank you. Yes, please, whatever you can do."

"How do I get in touch with you if I find anything out?"

He thought about that for a minute and then said, "It's probably better if I contact you. Why don't you give me your cell-phone number and I'll call you in a few days."

So, I gave him my number and promised to find out something as quickly as I could.

When I got home later that night, my family must have thought I was crazy. I was so glad to see them. I was thankful that nothing had befallen them like that poor man, Travis.

Even over dinner, when I found out that Alexandra had been disciplined for acting up in school, I didn't say one word. I just smiled and nodded. I treasured every moment with them that night.

The next morning as I drove to my office, the sky looked so beautiful and yet at the same time so ominous. I had been able to put the war out of my conscious like most people I suppose, but then between the Super Soldier experiments and this stuff with Travis, my heart had felt heavy.

As soon as I arrived at my office, I put in a call to Frank Alfaro. His assistant put me through to him. Through our conversation, he told me that it would be better if he had Eric King talk to me as Eric was directly familiar with the situation. Eric King was the director of special projects in military intelligence back then. He said that he'd notify Eric and have him meet me later.

So, I went about my daily business wondering about this guy Travis. I actually thought about calling you, Wes, to see if you knew anything about it, but on second thought decided it was best to wait for Eric.

Around three o'clock, Eric poked his head into my outer office. I saw him and waved him in. He must have come straight from the Pentagon as he was still wearing his colonel's uniform.

"Go ahead and have a seat," I said and got up to close the door.

"Sorry it took me awhile to get back to you. I'm sure from what this guy, Travis told you, you must've been waiting on pins and needles," Eric said as he sat.

"Do you need anything? Some water perhaps?" I asked Eric before we began.

"No, I'm fine. We better just get to it. Bottom line is this guy is certifiable. It's a given that this conversation is classified, right?"

"Of course."

"Okay, my people tell me that Travis Cage did in fact work for them but not anymore. He's gone rogue. He was working on some new ways to help our injured soldiers in the field using this new technology developed by one of our other teams. But it turns out that he was really an anti-war nut. He started working on his own project in secret. He intended to blackmail the government into stopping the war," King said in one explosive breath.

"I can't believe this. He seemed so sincere. What

about his daughter?" I asked shocked.

"It's all a lie. She's not the one who's infected. He is. I personally spoke to the head of the project, Dr. Wilhelm. He told me that somehow during Cage's unauthorized experiments he infected himself. He said that Cage is living on borrowed time."

Eric must have seen the look of horror on my face because he grasped my shoulder and asked me, "Is everything all right? You look like someone stepped on your grave."

"No, I'm all right, it's just that... Well, last night, he touched me with his hand. He isn't contagious is he?"

Understanding dawned on Eric and he said, "No, you have nothing to worry about. He wasn't working on anything communicable. If he had been we'd have put a dragnet out for him long ago."

I was confused. "So why doesn't he just turn himself in and get some help?"

"The stuff he's done amounts to treason. He's facing fifty years in Leavenworth, if not the death penalty. My guess is if he figures he can find a cure, then he can escape."

My head was spinning and some of what Eric was saying wasn't adding up, but I had no reason to doubt someone the Secretary of Defense had sent. "Well, I gave him my number. What should I do when he calls?"

Eric pulled a business card from his wallet and quickly scribbled a number on the back of it. He handed the card to me and said, "This is the number of the lead investigator on the Cage case. When Travis calls you, set up a meet and then call this investigator. Give him the details of your meeting and we'll pick him up."

I hesitated a moment and then took the card. I

needed time to think. Maybe gather more information. I wasn't sure at all as to what I'd do when the moment arose.

"Well, I have to get back. My wife is pregnant, with twins no less, and gets a little worried when I'm out too late. Thanks for notifying us about this guy. Man, is he bad news," King said slowly rising.

I mumbled some sort of goodbye and barely noticed as he left.

It took me awhile but eventually I was able to get back to work and take my mind off all the doom, gloom and conspiracies.

Late that night after Alex had been tucked in and Greg had wandered off to bed, I found myself in my study nursing a glass of Cabernet.

The house was still. I could hear the ticking of the grandfather clock against the wall and the howling of the wind outside my window. Their sounds portended something ominous.

There was a swallow or two left in the glass but I'd had enough. I stood up from my leather chair intending to go to bed when the phone on my desk rang. I picked it up quickly so the noise wouldn't wake Alex or Greg and said, "Hello."

"Hi, Senator," Travis said, "Did you find anything out? Anyway to help my little girl?"

I nearly jumped at the sound of his voice. My own voice quivered as I asked him, "How did you get my home number? And is it safe for you to be calling me like this?"

"Remember, I work for military intelligence? I've got a scrambler and jammer on this line. If anybody's tracing this call, they think it's coming from China somewhere. And if they're listening all they're hearing is static."

He laughed then. It was arrogant and completely

out of place given the seriousness of the situation, I thought.

Wes thought back to when he met Travis in the alley. Yes, he had heard that laugh. But Wes couldn't help but wonder if that wasn't arrogance as much as the inner mental workings of a person too smart for their own good. After all, how many times had Wes been told how arrogant his own laugh sounded?

"Yes, I found an ambassador at the U.N. who is a scientist and specializes in Human Rights violations," I lied. "He's a Swedish diplomat and says he may be able to get you and your daughter into his country as political refugees but he needs to meet you first."

Right then I decided that Travis was lying about his daughter and I was going to turn him in.

There was silence on the other end of the phone for a long time. Once again I could clearly hear the clock's ticking and the wind howling. Finally, I asked, "Travis... Travis... Are you there?"

"Yes, yes, I'm here. It's just that I'm so overwhelmed. I knew you were the right one for me to approach about this. Thank you. Thank you. When can I meet him?"

"He's still doing some business at the Capitol before heading back to New York. So, I'll meet you and then we can both meet him for lunch. Let's say 11 a.m. at the downtown shopping mall?"

"And where, exactly?" Travis said barely containing the excitement in his voice.

"There's a fountain in the middle of the main courtyard."

"Yes, I know the one."

"Meet me there," I said.

"Thanks again. You don't know what this means to me. I'll see you tomorrow. Sorry to call so late.

Have a good night," he said and then hung up before I could reply.

I downed the last of my wine and swallowed hard. The bitter, tangy liquid in my mouth tasted how I felt.

I reached into my study drawer and retrieved Eric King's card. I took a deep breath and then dialed.

Halfway through the first ring, the investigator answered. I told him where and when the meet was. I was about to go into how Travis had called me at home but he brushed it off. He either knew or didn't care. He politely thanked me and then hung up. Belatedly I wondered if the investigator was really a CIA agent whose assignment might be to kill Travis as opposed to capturing him. But it was too late.

The next day I found myself standing at the mall's fountain glancing at my watch for the fourth or fifth time. It read: 11:15 a.m., but there was no sign of Travis.

I paced back and forth in front of the fountain. I glanced around looking to see if I could spot the investigator. With no luck, I quickly gave up and was about to look at my watch again when my cell-phone rang.

"Hello. Is that you, Travis?" I answered.

At first the line was silent, then there was a blare of static and I heard him laugh. I think that laugh is burned into my psyche. I don't think I'll ever forget it. He asked me, "Do you think I'm a fool, Senator?"

Damn! I thought to myself. Somehow he'd found out about the trap. But I still feigned ignorance.

"What are you talking about? I..."

"Don't lie to me, Senator!" he yelled at me. "Do you think I'd be so gullible as to not even check out the little yarn you spun for me? The Swedish ambassador is a *she*, not a he. And *she* is currently on vacation. The deputy ambassador is filling in for her. When you make up lies, you should at least base them on a semblance of the truth."

"I'm sorry, Travis," I sputtered. "I spoke to the Secretary of Defense and his assistant, Eric King. They said you're the one who needs help. They just want you to come in."

"Really? Then I suppose the sniper they've got posted on the roof of that tall, bank building to the east over there is just to do some target practice on birds?" Travis asked.

I shielded my eyes and looked to the roof of the bank building. I didn't see anyone but I didn't doubt someone was up there.

"I'm sorry, Travis," I repeated. "I just don't know what to think."

"You should've trusted me. Really, think about it. What would it have cost you to find out the truth?"

I had no response to that so he continued, "I can tell you this though Senator. If I somehow make it out of all this alive, you're going to pay. I'm going to make you remember this moment forever and regret that you didn't help my little girl. You're going to pay. You're all going to pay," he said and then the phone went dead.

A couple who had been sitting at one of the food court tables near the fountain, suddenly jumped up out of their seats. The woman pulled what looked like a walkie-talkie out of her coat and started shouting into it as she ran west. The man didn't move. He looked up toward the east, raised his arm above his head and twirled his index finger. Seconds later a helicopter flew overhead, heading west, too.

I thought, so that's where the agents were; in

plain sight. I'd looked right at and past them. But I bet Travis hadn't.

"And that's the last I ever heard of Travis Cage until just a couple of weeks ago," the Senator said to Wes upon finishing her tale.

"So, Dr. Wilhelm was the head of the project. What did he call it, Quicksand?" Wes asked.

"Yes, Quicksand," the Senator replied.

"Why didn't you just tell us?" Yumiko asked angrily. "If we had known about Travis before, we could have set up a stakeout. We could've caught him before he got near the King girls or Halli Alfaro."

"I know, I know!" the Senator yelled. "Don't you think I blame myself enough already for all of this? But even if I had wanted to, I couldn't have said anything."

"What are you talking about? It's your daughter," Wes said angrily.

"She's talking about Dr. Wilhelm. When Travis infected the doctor's daughter, he probably knew what it was right away. When he got that hourglass, that confirmed it for him; Project Quicksand. He had his daughter cremated and himself as well so there'd be no evidence. The Senator is talking about duty to one's country. No matter how misguided," Yumiko said.

"Is she right?" Wes asked Cole.

"What do you think would happen, Wes, if the world found out what we were working on? The wars are gone but not forgotten. There would be an uproar. We'd be brought before the U.N. and charged for war crimes for even working on a biological weapon like that, much less using it.

"America would lose all of what's left of our shredded credibility. We'd probably find a way to wriggle out of it like we always do, but all those old wounds would be ripped open again."

"And you'd sacrifice your own daughter for that?" Wes asked in disbelief. "Will she be cremated, too? Will all of these people here today see your daughter in a coffin or in a little silver urn?"

"That's not fair! You of all people should know that wasn't my intent. But if you want to put it that way, then yes, I would and I did sacrifice my own flesh and blood to protect this country. Karl, explain it to them. They just don't get it," the Senator said throwing up her hands in disgust.

Karl stood up from the bench and said, "When we got attacked on 9/11, it was for no other reason than the terrorists hated our way of life; our freedoms and our culture. An ideological reason. Now, imagine what they'd do if they had a legitimate reason?"

The tension from the back and forth, made Wes' ribs start to ache so he sat down on one of the stone benches. He put the palms of his hands on the cool stone, enjoying the earthy feeling.

"Even though I'm sure you believe that, Karl, it still doesn't excuse the cover-up. Let me put it like this. What if we found out that the Middle-East or China had a secret genetic weapon designed to wipe out white Americans? Would we allow them to keep their secret to preserve the peace? Or would we want the world to know?" Wes asked.

"If keeping Americans in the dark would keep them safe, then we should allow them their secrets. You have no idea about what it takes, Wes. You're a smart guy, but most Americans aren't as rational or practical as you. They don't want the truth, they want to be safe," Brooks countered.

"Look you boys can debate this later all you want. Right now there's a killer out there intent on doing more harm. Specifically, to your own daughter, Karl," Yumiko said as she stepped between Wes and Brooks. "Now, what I want to know... No, what I need to know is, what is your part in this? Dr. Wilhelm, the Senator here, King, and Defense Secretary Alfaro were all involved directly or indirectly with Cage and Project Quicksand. Why is he after you?"

"Yeah, come to think of it, he had a message for you, too, Brooks," Wes added. "He told me to tell you he was doing your daughter, Serena, a favor. What did he mean by that?"

Brooks looked down at his hands and picked at his fingernails while he considered his options. Finally, he raised his head and looking into Yumiko's eyes said, "Okay. I met Cage before, too. After Senator Cole met him, in fact."

Yumiko, not surprised in the least, only nodded.

———————

I was an up and coming agent at the time. I had just become a field supervisor and was in line to supervise a whole region.

I don't know why he approached me. My guess is he knew of me from some of the more, flashy and high profile cases I'd been involved in.

Anyway, I remember it was in December. I had finished up a round of golf and went to my office to do some work. I had wanted to finish up some casework before meeting my wife for lunch.

I liked working on Sundays. I still do. It's quiet. You can think through problems without the hustle and bustle of other agents around. Or a bunch of people intruding on your space with stupid questions. I probably solved more of my cases on

Sundays than any other time of the week.

So, I walked into the dimly lit building and made my way to my office. The blinds were closed and in the poor illumination I didn't see him sitting in the corner, at first.

When I flipped on the light, I caught him in my peripheral vision. I pulled out my sidearm and whipped around. I thought it was an ambush. I would've put a bullet in him if he had moved even one inch. But he didn't. Looking back now, it probably would've been better for everyone if he had. But like I said, he didn't. He just stared at me.

I realize now that his daughter's death had made him a shell of a man. That and he was worn out from the military hounding him like a dog. Yeah, that's kinda how he looked; like a beaten dog.

When Cole saw him, he was nervous and jumpy but when I met him, his movements were slow and deliberate. His overcoat was filthy. His face was scruffy and dirty. His eyes were bloodshot and had bags under them. He looked like he hadn't slept or eaten in days.

He said, "I'm sorry, I didn't mean to scare you."

"Who are you and how did you get in here?" I asked him.

"Name's Jones. Snuck in with the janitors on Friday night. Been hiding here ever since," he replied.

I don't know why he bothered to lie. He had to have known that we would've had his wanted poster and profile. His bio indicated that he was a high-value domestic terrorist.

As I studied him, his eyes seemed to say, "this is my last hope." Perhaps he thought I'd have some sympathy for him or maybe his mind was gone. Either way, I played along. I mean, I had him. I could've taken him in to the military at any second and after that, the sky was the limit in my career.

I holstered my weapon. I helped him off the floor and sat him in a chair. "It's okay, Jones, you're safe. Nobody's going to hurt you."

He sighed heavily seemingly relieved by my words.

"Do you need anything to drink? Or maybe something to eat?" I asked him.

He shook his head, but I scrounged up some coffee and a pastry from the lounge's vending machine anyway.

When I gave the food to him, he wolfed it down without even bothering to chew or taste it. It was like he just needed the fuel to keep his body going.

I pulled up a chair in front of him and sat down. I said, "Okay, now that we've got your belly filled, what can I do for you, Jones? Why are you here?"

"Experiments," Travis said haltingly.

"What about experiments?" I prodded.

"I'm homeless. Lost my job a while back. Been living on the streets. In the night they come sometimes and take away some of the people," he said.

This guy is crazy, I thought. He was getting more and more paranoid with every passing second. He was seeing conspiracies around every corner. I asked, "What people? Who's doing this?"

"The other homeless people. They're being taken away by the government and experimented on," he said darkly.

"Where did this happen? What proof or evidence do you have?" I asked. I didn't really care about his flight of fantasy but I was establishing trust between us. I even grabbed a pad and pencil and pretended to take notes.

"It's a place under a bridge where a lot of the homeless live. Almost a tent city. They come at night in black vans and take them away," Travis said.

"Okay, if it's not too far, let's go and check it out," I said.

Travis seemed surprised that I was so eager to investigate. His eyes actually flickered with some signs of life.

He said, "Oh... oh... okay. Yes, I can show you where. Thank you."

"Thanks for what," I asked.

"For... believing in me," he replied softly.

I shook my head. "No, thank you. I can tell you've seen something. Something people need to know about. We'll get to the bottom of this. I guarantee it.

"Wait here a second, I'll be right back and then we can go."

When I returned I had another vending machine Danish and cup of coffee for him.

"Okay, let's go," I said and escorted him to my car that was parked out front.

Once we were on our way I said, "So, where exactly is this place?"

Travis sipped his coffee and answered, "I don't have an address or anything like that. I know it by landmarks."

"What's the most prominent landmark you remember?" I asked.

"You know the old town mall?"

"Yes, the one that used to have the big blue sign you could see from the freeway? That one?"

"Yes, that's the one. Head there. When we get over there I can direct you the rest of the way," Travis said and then took another sip of the hot coffee.

"I got it. Now, you just relax, Jones," I said. "We're going to get to the bottom of all this. Trust me."

Travis stared at me then for a few seconds. His eyelids started to droop and he turned away. A moment later he passed out. I was able to just grab the coffee cup before the last of it spilled on him. I set the cup in the holder and pulled over.

I checked Travis' pulse to make sure he was okay. It was strong and steady. I was worried that maybe I had given him too many sleeping pills but I hadn't.

I pulled out my cell-phone and called the number that had been written on the terrorist bulletin. Like the Senator said, halfway through the first ring someone picked up.

I said, "I'm Karl Brooks, FBI field supervisor. I've got Travis Cage."

The voice on the other end didn't seem surprised or pleased by my information. He only said, "Your location?"

I gave it to him and he said, "One moment."

The line went silent while I waited.

When he came back on the line the man said, "Take him to 1335 Watercrest Way. It is approximately ten minutes from your current location. Do you need directions?"

"No, I know that area. Is that a safe house or something?" I asked.

Instead of answering my question the voice said, "If you encounter any resistance, retreat to a safe location and notify us immediately. Otherwise we will be expecting you in ten minutes."

Then the line went dead.

I started the car up and pulled back onto the deserted street.

As I drove, I berated myself for acting like a rookie. I couldn't believe I was asking dumb questions. Of course the location I was taking Travis to was a safe house.

Ten minutes later, I pulled up in front of 1335 Watercrest Way. It was a pastel yellow single-story house, in a suburban neighborhood. The yard was well-kept but the house itself was dark. Being Sunday there weren't any cars or people out and about in the immediate area.

I stepped out of the car and the house's front door immediately flew open. Two big men, one white and the other black, both wearing casual clothes, emerged from the house. They moved toward me and the car. Without even acknowledging me, they opened up the passenger seat, grabbed Travis, and carried him back into the house.

I locked up my car and quickly followed them inside.

When I entered, the door shut behind me. The African-American man who'd come outside had been standing behind it. He smiled briefly at me and then gestured for me to continue on into the house proper.

By the time I had gotten into the living room, the white guy I'd seen was already strapping Travis down into a heavy, oak chair.

The man stepped back to admire his handiwork when it was complete. He turned and smiled at me, but said nothing. We were waiting for something.

Not wanting to come off like a rookie again, I waited in silence also. I took the opportunity to glance around the room.

It was sparsely furnished. It had just the right amount of furniture to perhaps fool a nosy neighbor but the illusion would fall apart on closer inspection.

For example, there weren't any photos of the supposed family who might live there.

After another ten minutes passed, the second man suddenly cocked his head as if he was listening to something. Seconds later we could hear the front door open and then, shut.

A tall, Asian man in his thirties entered the living room. His light sweater, jeans and dress boots hung loosely on his medium-built frame.

The white man nodded to the newcomer and stepped back out of the way. The Asian gentleman was apparently the one we'd been waiting for.

He turned to me, stuck out his hand and said, "Good work, Brooks. Name's Walter."

I shook his hand and said, "Thanks."

"What did you give him?"

"Lorazepam. We keep some as part of our medical kit. I slipped a double dose into his coffee. He hadn't eaten in awhile so it took effect almost immediately," I said.

Walter nodded and checked his watch. I guessed he was calculating how long Travis would be out.

"How did you capture him?"

"I usually work on Sundays. I went to my office awhile ago and there he was waiting for me. He said that he'd snuck in with the cleaning crew last Friday and had been there ever since," I said and shrugged.

Walter smiled at me and nodded. "Why you?"

Walter's pinpoint accurate questions were starting to unnerve even me and I was on his side. I could understand why he was in charge, though. I replied, "I'm not sure. Other than I worked on the Glenn serial killings last year. It was all over the media."

He checked his watch and looked at Travis again. "Yes, I remember that case. Very high-profile."

I shrugged. "I guess."

Walter turned and looked me in the eyes coldly as he said, "Well, this is very low-profile. You can stay, but keep your mouth shut. You might learn a thing or two and advance your career at the same time. If you can't handle that, there's the door."

I hesitated less than a second before I said, "I can handle it."

Walter smiled at me. Then, with a furious backhand, he slapped Travis hard. The sound of it was like a gunshot.

Travis came instantly awake, sputtering and coughing. He shook his head and when he realized where he was, he looked at us with unadulterated hate.

Walter bent in close to Travis and said, "You've been a naughty boy, Cage. Are we going to have a polite conversation or is Andy here going to have to gag you?"

Travis looked at the second man called Andy and looked back to Walter. Travis mumbled something underneath his breath. Walter bent in closer and said, "Sorry, Cage, didn't catch that?"

Like a snake, Travis shot his neck forward and bit into Walter's cheek. Andy stepped forward and clubbed Travis on the head as Walter tore away.

"I said, I'm going to kill you first, Walter," Travis said and spat Walter's blood on the light-colored carpet.

Walter threw back his head and roared laughter. "That's the spirit, Cage. Get my bag out of the car Andy and tell Rod to get in here."

Andy disappeared and Rod promptly entered the living room.

"This dog bites. Gag him," Walter ordered Rod.

Rod produced a handkerchief out of nowhere like a magician. Travis whipped his head back and forth to avoid the handkerchief but Rod was able to hold his head still long enough to gag him.

Holding his right cheek with his hand to staunch the flow of blood, Walter turned to me and said, "Okay, hero, let's see what you've got. Tune him up."

"What?" I asked at first not comprehending.

"I want to hear some singing, Brooks. Now tune him up. Unless you don't care that this man has attacked a superior officer?" Walter commanded. "You are still in the reserves, aren't you?"

I'd been in on plenty of interrogations where we knew the perp was guilty as hell but just wouldn't give it up. And without the evidence at hand, they would've walked if we hadn't tuned them up as Walter put it.

But this case seemed different. I mean we hadn't even asked the guy any questions, yet.

I looked at Travis who was glaring at me. If looks could kill, I would've fallen dead right on the spot.

I looked at Walter who said, "Do you hear that, Rod?"

The black agent shook his head and said, "No, sir."

"How about you, Andy?" Walter asked the other agent who'd just returned with Walter's medical bag.

"No, sir," Andy replied as he handed the bag to Walter.

Walter reached in the bag and pulled out some gauze as he said, "I hear a flushing sound. I hear the sound of Brooks' career here going down the toilet."

As he patted his cheek with the gauze, Walter stared at me.

I rolled up my sleeves and tuned Travis up.

When Walter was done patching up his cheek,

he ordered me to stop. It'd been awhile since I'd done something like that so my knuckles were sore and a slight sweat had broken out on my brow.

A cut had sprung up over Travis' left eyebrow but he took the pain well. Other than a grunt or two, there'd been almost no reaction from him.

Walter nodded his approval. He bent in to Travis again and asked him, "Still feel like biting?"

Travis looked at Walter warily.

Walter stood up and said, "No, I didn't think so."

With a nod from Walter, Rod reached over and removed Travis' gag. He looked at Travis with pity seeing one of his own brethren treated like that but he was a soldier and kept any objections he had to himself.

Travis didn't yell or scream, he just turned to me and said, "He's first and you'll be last Brooks."

Walter only laughed at that but I could see in Travis' eyes that he meant every word. I doubted he'd get away from the government again, but if he ever got the opportunity, I was sure he'd try to kill me."Now, where is the serum, Cage?" Walter asked. "We know you stole a sample. We can't have that stuff floating around."

Travis looked at Walter but remained quiet.

"No? The data then. We've retraced your steps. We know you did a data dump as well, before you left. Where'd you put those files, Cage?" Walter persisted.

Still Travis said nothing.

Walter smiled and reached for his bag. He withdrew a syringe and a vial of clear liquid. As he used the syringe to draw fluid from the vial he said, "You're going to talk one way or another, Cage."

"You first, Brooks last," Travis repeated.

And after that, even though we worked on him

for hours, he never said another word. I had to give
the guy credit. They did everything short of sticking
needles underneath his fingernails to get him to talk
but he never did.

"And you participated in that?" Yumiko hissed at
Brooks.

"I did what I had to, it was a matter of national
security," Brooks replied.

Yumiko and Brooks began shouting back and
forth then. It went on for a little while before Wes
and Cole were able to calm the situation back down.

"Now if you two can stop fighting for two
seconds, we still have some unanswered question
here," Wes said. "For example, if the government
had him when you left him, Brooks, how did he end
up faking his own death?"

Brooks took a deep breath and said, "From what
I was told, his condition deteriorated after that
drastically. He was taken to a secure infirmary for
observation. Shortly after arriving there, he
disguised himself as a nurse and escaped. About a
week after that, they found his body at the bottom of
a cliff."

"Weren't you the least bit concerned that the guy
might've been telling the truth? Weren't you worried
that you might've been wrong? I mean, you've told
me a thousand times about proper procedure and
making a good bust. What happened to all of that?"
Yumiko demanded.

Brooks looked at Yumiko and Wes defiantly as
he said, "No, I wasn't concerned. After I walked out
of that safe house, I never even gave Travis Cage a
second thought. I was doing my job. And everything
I've ever told you Yumiko about the job is still true. I
believe absolutely that what I did in that room was
the right thing. And If I had it to do all over again, I'd

do the exact same thing."

Wes stretched and then pointed at Brooks as he said, "Now I see what he meant. You're a monster, Brooks. You've become what you hate most. He'd be doing your daughter a favor by killing her rather than have her be raised by someone like you."

Brooks lunged at Wes yelling, "Damn you!"

Before he could get close though, Yumiko stuck out a foot and Brooks tripped on it, falling to the ground.

When Brooks stood up, his face was red and flushed. He was literally shaking as he pointed at Wes and said, "That's it. I hope you've enjoyed it because that's it. That's all you're going to get. Yumiko, you're reinstated. Now, arrest him."

Cole and Yumiko looked at Brooks in disbelief. Senator Cole said, "Karl, you can't be serious. He's trying to save your daughter."

"He thinks I'm a monster. So, maybe I am. I don't need his kind of help. Look in his eyes. You can see that he sympathizes with this serial killer, Travis. He might as well be the killer himself," Brooks said with spittle flying from his mouth as he shouted.

"On what charges?" Yumiko asked still not believing what she was hearing.

"As a material witness. Nobody's interviewed him yet on what happened in that alley when he was allegedly attacked," Brooks practically screeched. "Now take him into custody."

"Come on, sir, you've got to be kidding right. I mean I just found out that Travis' mother had a farm that's never been sold or torn down. We're pretty sure he's operating out of that farm but I'll need Wes' help," Yumiko pleaded.

"Good work, Yumiko. You'll be in charge of the second tactical team that'll make an insertion on the farm. I'll lead the first strike team. But he's out. I'm done with this condescending bastard. Now take him to the detention center back at the Annex or I'll get another agent who will," Brooks said looking at Yumiko coolly.

Brooks could've gotten another agent to take Wes and knew he should've but in a way, Wes was right. Brooks would never admit it to himself, but in that safe house all those long years ago, he had discovered he'd *enjoyed* watching Travis Cage being tortured. And now as he ordered Yumiko to put Wes in custody, he relished the fact that he'd be shredding whatever bond of friendship that he could see brewing between the two. He'd be putting the screws to Wes and Yumiko at the same time. He kept his expression stone-faced but inside he was laughing as Yumiko grasped Wes by his upper arm.

"Come on Wes, let's go," Yumiko said. "It's bullshit and we'll find a way to get you out of this, but for now, let me take you downtown. It'll be easier this way."

To Brooks, Wes said," You're going to regret this."

David Underwood paused at the foyer's mailbox and checked for his mail before taking the stairs up to his third floor apartment.

He was getting on in years and his knees ached from time to time. They especially bothered him on a day like today when he'd been on his feet for eight hours straight. He would've taken the elevator except it didn't work right half the time.

When he reached the third floor landing, he made his way to the end of the weakly lit hall. It was only 3:30 in the afternoon but the office buildings that crowded around his small apartment building blocked out what was left of the overcast sunlight.

At the end of the hall, he pulled his keys out of his pocket and picked through them until he found the right one. He glanced up at his door. 310 stood out in chipped, bronze numerals. David sighed heavily and his once powerful shoulders sagged in defeat. He inserted the key and turned it in the lock.

He pushed the door open and stepped into darkness. That's odd, David thought. He always left the table lamp over by the window on when he left in the morning. The landlord had never fixed the hallway light and David didn't like having to fumble around in the darkness. All he would need would be to fall and break his neck.

David sighed and dropped the bag with his uniform in it next to the door. He then felt along the wall and around it to the lamp. His vision had slowly become adjusted to the light. What's that in my good chair? He asked himself as he reached for the switch on the lamp and turned it.

As light flooded the room, David realized that the object in his good chair was a man. An African-American man like himself but this man was younger and he was holding a pistol.

"Don't move, David, or call out. I'm not here to hurt you," Travis said from the comfort of the leather easy chair.

David was almost sure the man was a drug addict come to steal his stuff and kill him. He wanted to scream or lift up the lamp and bash the intruder's brains in, but he just didn't have that much personal violence in himself anymore. His shoulders sagged deeper at the thought of his own impotence.

"Don't hurt me," David said. "You can take

whatever valuables I got. I ain't gon' tell nobody. Just don't hurt me."

Travis smiled a sad smile and said, "Please shut the door, slowly, and then sit, Mr. Underwood. Like I said, I'm not going to hurt you. I need something from you. Actually, I need three things from you. The gun was just to get your attention. I would've approached you differently but time is always against me these days. It above all is my greatest enemy, I suppose."

This guy doesn't talk like any drug addict I ever heard, David thought to himself. As the man had requested, David went back and shut the door. He then took the less comfortable but sturdy wood and fabric chair across from the intruder.

"Well, if you ain't here to steal from me. What you want, son? This here can't lead to nothing but trouble," David reasoned.

"You've got that right, Mr. Underwood. My name's Travis by the way. When this is all over, you might hear that name on TV or see it in the papers. They're probably gonna say some bad things about me, Mr. Underwood, but you don't believe it. No, sir. You don't believe one word," Travis said as he shifted the pistol and pointed it at the floor.

"So, you want to *borrow* some money?" David guessed.

"No, sir. I want to borrow *you*. Just for a day though," Travis replied.

David shook his head. "I'm not following you Travis. You're gonna have to explain that one."

"Sorry, it's been a long time since I've actually sat and spoken to someone. I'm used to talking to myself. And sometimes the TV. You'll have to bear with me as I get the hang of it again," Travis said, again smiling sadly.

David didn't know this man, Travis, from a hole in the wall and yet, he felt sorry for him. It was obvious that Travis had been through a lot. Probably as much or more as David had gone through back in Vietnam.

"Well, take your time, son," David said. "I ain't got nowhere I got to be."

Travis sucked in a deep cleansing breath and blew it out. "Thanks Mr. Underwood, I appreciate that. Okay, to put it simply, I need to borrow your security badge and your uniform. I'm also going to need to tie you up and leave you in this apartment for at least eight hours. Maybe longer. I'm going to impersonate you tomorrow."

"Do you know where I work, Travis? At the FBI. I'm the head custodian. Been working for them goin' on ten years now. Pretending to be me will get you jail time." David said shocked at what he'd heard. "You seem to be an educated and sophisticated young brother. Why you wanna try some fool stunt like that? You ain't no Oklahoma City bomber or something crazy like that, are you?"

Travis had to laugh at that. "No, I'm not going to blow up the building, Mr. Underwood. I am going to get my pound of flesh though."

"Pound of flesh? Somebody in that building done you wrong?" David asked.

Travis nodded slowly. "Yes, sir. Me and my baby girl. She's gone because of some bad men and their experiments."

"Experiments..." David said, thinking back on his own past. "Like Agent Orange...?"

"Yes, like that, Mr. Underwood, but much, much worse."

"I don't know, Travis..." David said as he pushed himself up from his chair. "My momma always say, if

you set out for revenge, you best start by diggin' two
graves."

The gun in Travis' hand snapped to attention
and remained trained on the old Vietnam vet as he
made his way to his kitchenette. David took note of
that as he bent and opened the fridge.

"Beer?" he called out.

"No, thanks," Travis replied as David proceeded
to get himself one. David tore off the cap with the
magnetic bottle opener stuck to the fridge door.

David opened the cabinet under the sink where
he kept a trash bin. It was also the place he kept his
sawed-off shotgun.

As he tossed the bottle cap into the trash, he
quickly felt behind the sink's pipes for his secret
weapon but it was gone.

He closed the cabinet doors and went back into
the living room.

When David was again comfortably seated with
his beer in hand, Travis let the pistol droop toward
the floor.

"Well, you tell me, Mr. Underwood," Travis said.
"If someone could have stopped the Vietnam War
before all those young boys died, or the Iraq War or
any war for that matter, wouldn't it be worth it?
Wouldn't it be worth a couple of government officials
suffering for the whole world to be free?"

"No one should have to suffer..." David
suggested as he took a sip of his cold beer.

"That's right," Travis agreed. "If you had a time
machine and could go back into the past and kill
Hitler when he was born, would you do it? Well, I
have that time machine right now. Are you going to
tell me I shouldn't use it?"

"I can see you're a smart man, Travis, probably a
whole lot smarter than me, but how can you be sure?

How can you be so sure that what you're doing is right? Remember, pride goeth before the fall?" David countered.

"Because I worked for them. I helped make the weapon that someday is going to kill everyone on this planet if they're not careful. I'd tell you more but when they come looking for you, they're going to ask you questions. Questions it'd be best if you *didn't* know the answers to," Travis insisted.

"Well if you mean to tie me up, take my things, and do this anyway, why're you even telling me all this?" David asked as he took another sip from his bottle.

Travis sighed and massaged his neck. He said, "I'm a dead man. One way or another. I suppose I just wanted what everyone wants–– understanding. After it's all over, I'd like one person to be able to say, 'I didn't agree with him, but I understood.'"

David finished the last half of his beer in one long draught. He let out a small, satisfying burp.

Then, he got up and went into the kitchenette. He noted the pistol in Travis' hand tracked him once again.

As he was throwing away his beer bottle in the trash beneath the sink, he thought that Travis was probably bat-shit crazy. Even after all David himself had gone through at the hands of the government, he couldn't believe half of what this Travis guy was saying. On the other hand, though, this Travis guy was also smart. He'd found and disposed of David's shotgun. He'd also found the perfect way to break into the FBI.

David went back out into the living room and sat back down. He looked over at the picture of his wife on the wall. She'd been gone ten years now. The big 'C' had gotten her. He looked at the pictures of his kids and grandkids who never had time for him anymore; never dropping by or even bothering to call. He looked at the yellowed photo of his old unit; all those soldiers gone now, except for himself.

He looked back to Travis who was nodding as if he'd been listening to David's thoughts as he'd let his old memories wash over him like so much rain. To Travis he said, "I think you're bat-shit crazy. I think what you're saying isn't anywhere near the truth. But I've done my time. Hell, I've done mine and then some. I'm due some overtime, as a matter of fact. So, no, I don't agree with you, but yeah, Travis, I understand."

Wednesday — December 8

After waking Wes up, Yumiko sat across from him on a metal stool. Wes' detention cell had once been an exam room when the FBI Annex had been a hospital. When it had been converted, they kept half of the basement hospital rooms and converted them into part infirmary and part detention area for suspects or prisoners.

Wes sat up on the uncomfortable cot and swung his socked feet over the side. He rubbed his jaw absent-mindedly as he glanced around at the white walls.

Yumiko handed him a cup of hot coffee. He was thirsty and sipped it a little too quickly which resulted in a slightly burned tongue. He took the lid off and set the cup on the floor next to his cot to cool.

"So, how are the King girls doing? It's been three days now. They're running out of time," Wes said as he rubbed the sleep from his eyes.

"Not well. Even though they're twins, they're reacting to the infection quite differently," Yumiko sighed. "Tisha is being affected much more quickly. Late last night, they had to put her into the intensive care unit after she began having heart palpitations."

"Damn!" Wes yelled as he punched his palm

with his fist. "What's Brooks thinking locking me up like this?"

Wes got up and moved to the door. He looked out of the glass window onto an empty, fluorescent bulb lit hall. Wes knew there was a guard that patrolled from time to time, but didn't see him now. The guard was probably back at his station in front of the elevators. That's where Wes had seen him before when they brought him in. That same guard would come around and let Yumiko out when she pressed the buzzer next to the door.

Yumiko shook her head. "I can't even begin to imagine. Unless it's true what they say about power corrupting people. I think he started out with good intentions but got his ambition confused with his duty."

"Yeah, and now everyone else has to pay for his mistakes."

"Well, it's not entirely his fault. If not for Alfaro, King and whoever else came up with this crazy idea there'd be no Travis Cage. I think there's plenty of blame to be spread around," Yumiko suggested.

"That's true. It's just that I was getting close. I know it. I could feel it. I'm beginning to understand how Travis thinks. If I wasn't locked up down here, I know I could put the pieces together," Wes lamented.

"Well, you won't be completely out of the loop," Yumiko said as she reached into a bag she'd brought with her. "I convinced the brass that you could still be useful. They allowed me to give you back your laptop so you can keep working. The whole place is wi-fied so you don't need a hard line, but your access has been severely limited."

Yumiko handed Wes the computer from her bag.

"What if I need something that I'm not able to

access directly?" Wes asked as he moved from the window to set the laptop on the cot. He bent down, picked up the now cooler coffee and took a sip.

"Your access has been restricted to the FBI intranet so although you can't send or receive emails from the outside, you can still send them internally. If you need anything, email me or Martin and we'll do our best to get you what you need. That's also how I'll keep you posted on our mission at the Cage farm," Yumiko replied.

"They've already got your tactical team ready to go?" Wes asked.

"Just about. I'm going to brief everyone on the mission in ten minutes. I just wanted to stop in and check on you. And let you know that we can still use your help," Yumiko said, standing.

"Thanks, I appreciate it. And since you mentioned it, I already have a request," Wes said.

"Sure, anything."

Wes had to pause at the way she phrased that and then he said, "Remember when Brooks told us that Travis had said he'd be the last?"

"Yes, I remember that. What did you make of it?"

"Well, from what we've seen of Travis and what my instincts tell me, Travis is a man of his word. If he said Brooks will be the last, he'll do whatever possible to make that come true.

"Likewise, though, he said that Walter would be the first. I need you or Martin to find out about this Walter person."

Yumiko was nodding. "You think Walter is dead. And if we can find out where or when, that might give us more clues."

"Bingo," Wes said pointing a finger at Yumiko.

"Okay, I'll tell Martin to get right on it and send

you anything he finds. I'll check in with you in a couple of hours to get an update on your progress," Yumiko said as she reached for and pressed the buzzer.

Moments later, the guard showed up and let Yumiko out of the room. Once outside the room, Yumiko turned and glanced in the window. She gave Wes a quick warm smile and then disappeared. Wes shuddered. He had the unsettling feeling that he wasn't ever going to see her again.

———————

Travis carefully replaced the air conditioning vent he'd just come through.

Once he'd finished, he took a look around the janitorial room. There was a sink in the wall, three racks of shelves holding all manner of cleaning supplies, brooms, mops, brushes and there was a floor waxer/cleaner, too.

A rough plan had already been concocted by Travis before he even left David Underwood's apartment an hour ago. Being the genius he was however, always ready to adapt and capitalize on new information, Travis abandoned his previous plan and decided to go a different route.

First, he went to the mirror over the sink and checked his disguise. He'd scanned, altered and replaced the photo on Underwood's badge just enough to make it look more like himself in disguise. He had to admit that posing as Underwood was an extremely bold move. If he had run into anyone who knew Underwood well, his disguise would not have held up. Luck was on his side however, and he'd made it down into the infirmary basement without any trouble. The disguise still looked good, so Travis

went back over by the vent where he'd dropped
Underwood's bag.

He reached inside the bag and pulled out the
iPod that Underwood wore when he was cleaning up.
He put the iPod into the upper left pocket of his
work coveralls. Finally, he moved over to the floor
cleaner and studied its operation.

Confident from his review of the instructions
that he could operate the machine well enough to
fool any onlooker, Travis went to the door, unlocked
it and peeked out into the hallway

The hallway was empty, but Travis could hear
the distant sound of voices. Travis smiled and
nodded to himself before ducking back inside the
janitorial room.

The old plan had been for Travis to use a mop
and bucket to distract and confuse his enemies, but
upon seeing the floor cleaner, he'd decided that it
would be much more effective.

From his conversation with Underwood, Travis
knew that by going down this hall, through glass
double doors, and down another hall to the right, he
would be led to the guard stationed there. That
would be his primary objective. Then, the party
would really start.

Travis pushed the cleaner out into the hall. He
put the ear buds from the iPod into his ear. He began
bobbing his head and shuffling to an imaginary song.
Then, he flipped on the battery powered cleaner and
began pushing it down the hallway.

As expected, per Underwood's information,
when he got about halfway down the corridor, it
opened out onto a large room. The room had once
been used as a waiting room when the building had
been a hospital. The nurses' station still stood at the
end of the room, but was now empty. And now

instead of the many waiting chairs that had once been in the room, there were now only two sofas.

Seated in one of the sofas facing a television anchored to the opposite wall, were two teenagers. The girl on the left was Serena Brooks. Next to her on the right, was her brother Kevin. Travis' global positioning locator had been dead on the mark. Brooks had thought he could hide his daughter from Travis. Well, he had thought wrong, horribly wrong.

Sitting across from the two teenagers, on the other couch, were agents Abrams and Gonzalez.

And so, also as expected, as soon as Travis had come out from the hallway and into the open of the waiting room, Gonzalez had jumped up, drawn his gun and leveled it at Travis.

Abrams had jumped up and moved in front of the children to shield them from any potential threat.

Gonzalez yelled out, "Freeze! Stop right there!"

Travis pretended to not hear through the floor cleaner's noise. He also kept his head bobbing to the phantom beat, seemingly oblivious to Gonzalez' presence.

"I said freeze!" Gonzalez shouted out again as he transferred his grip from a two-handed one, to a one-handed one. Abrams had drawn her weapon as well.

With the television program forgotten, the kids had gotten up and moved behind Abrams' protective stance.

Having inched forward and with his left hand stretched out to Travis, Gonzalez pushed Travis' shoulder.

Travis jumped back and shouted out in mock surprise. He let go of the cleaner which careened into the middle of the room before stopping.

"What are you trying to do? Give an old man a heart attack?" Travis asked as he imitated Underwood's voice almost to perfection. "What y'all doing down here anyway?"

"No, sir, I'm asking the questions. I'm Agent Gonzalez. This area is restricted. What are you doing?"

"What was that?" Travis asked as he pretended to realize his earbuds were still in place.

Gonzalez repeated the question as Travis removed the earbuds. "I said, 'what are you doing in a restricted area?'"

"Look young buck, I've been the head custodian since you were in diapers. I think I know how to do my job," Travis said as if he'd been offended.

"I'm sure you do, Mr.?"

"Underwood. David Underwood."

"I'm sure you do, Mr. Underwood, but you're not supposed to be down here. Now please don't move. Abrams, can you confirm a Mr. Underwood for me?" Gonzalez said.

Gonzalez kept his gun low, but still trained on whom he thought was Mr. Underwood.

Travis shifted his profile from time to time to prevent Gonzalez from getting a really good look at his face.

The kids, who had been scared out of their wits during all the commotion had settled down somewhat and were whispering between themselves at the turn of events.

Finally, Abrams flipped her phone closed and nodded to Gonzalez. "He checks out okay."

Travis threw up his hands in exclamation. "See? What'd I tell you?"

Gonzalez lowered his gun even further and said, "Don't get in a huff, Mr. Underwood, we just had to make sure. But that still doesn't change the fact that you're not supposed to be in this area. I'd like for you to check in with the guard posted at the elevator and make arrangements to come back and clean this area some other time."

"No, problem, young buck. Sorry for any trouble I caused. Ma'am. Kids," Travis said with a nod as he gathered up his cleaning machine and rolled it toward the exit's double doors.

"Sorry about that, kids. I hope we didn't scare you too much," Gonzalez said as he holstered his weapon.

"No, it's okay and thanks," Serena said. "I was starting to get bored and miss my friends, but now I see what my Dad was talking about..."

"Yeah, you can't be too careful. There are a lot of..." Abrams trailed off as she sought the correct way to phrase her thought.

"Nut jobs?" Kevin suggested.

They all laughed at that.

"Yeah, I guess you could put it that way," Abrams said.

The kids had just settled back in to watching the TV when, to their surprise, the custodian came busting back in through the double doors.

"There's something wrong with your man! There's something wrong with your man!" Travis screamed as he ran into the middle of the room.

"Calm down, Mr. Underwood. What're you talking about?" Gonzalez commanded.

Travis took a huge deep breath, held it and then blew it out suddenly. He put a hand to his chest, as if to calm himself and then lowered it. He said, "I went to talk to the guard like you said, but I-I-I think he's dead. It looked like he was sleeping bent over but when I touched him, he didn't wake up and I saw the blood. That's when I came back in here."

In a flash, Gonzalez' sidearm was in his hand. "Watch the kids, Abrams and get on the horn to get some backup down here."

Abrams nodded her understanding that the killer had gained access to the basement and would be coming for them.

"Show me, Mr. Underwood," Gonzalez gestured.

"I ain't going back near some dead body. I'm staying here where it's safe," Travis protested.

"Fine. Stay here but don't move," Gonzalez ordered as he ran for the double doors.

Gonzalez sprinted down the corridor, around the corner and down the next corridor in record time. He covered the empty rooms with his weapon as he ran.

He approached the makeshift desk that had been set up for the security officer and sure enough, he could see the blood on the desk and the floor. He stepped closer, examining the body and any signs of the intruder at the same time. There was no sign of the killer, but Gonzalez clearly saw the handle of a scalpel sticking out of the back of the officer's neck.

Gonzalez heard what he thought was a gunshot. He realized what the sound meant and cursed himself for being an idiot. He quickly returned to the waiting room and burst through the double doors with his gun at the ready. Unfortunately, he was met by a disheartening sight.

Abrams was sprawled on a couch, holding one of her legs, which was bleeding. Kevin was next to her trying to help her with her wound.

Mr. Underwood, who Gonzalez had realized too late was really Travis Cage, was standing in the middle of the room with Serena shielding him. Travis was pointing Abrams' gun over Serena's shoulder with one hand and he had a scalpel to Serena's neck with the other.

Gonzalez skidded to a halt. "What the hell's going on here, Underwood?"

Back at Quantico, Gonzalez had been the number one sharpshooter in his class. He'd broken many of the FBI school's records. He could shoot the eye out of a bird at a 100 yards, but before he could get a bead on the killer, Travis shot Gonzalez. The sound of the shot echoed around the room. Serena screamed and Kevin put his hands to his ears.

Gonzalez dropped his weapon and fell back against the wall from the force of the blast. He clutched his shoulder and yelled out from the pain.

"You know what's going on, Gonzalez. Playing dumb won't work with me," Travis said.

"Cage..." Gonzalez said through pain gritted teeth.

"At your service," Travis said, "and you're Gonzalez. Now that introductions are over, let me say this: I've got no reason to kill you, so don't make me. That shot was just to disable you so you don't do anything foolish. Now kick your gun over here."

Gonzalez did as he was told.

"Kevin, pick up that gun and throw it in that trash bin over there," Travis commanded.

Kevin looked to Abrams who said, "Yeah, it's okay, Kevin. You can do what he says."

With his eyes darting back and forth from Travis to Abrams, Kevin walked to the gun and picked it up by the butt gingerly. He walked back over to the trash receptacle and gently dropped it inside.

"That's a good boy," Travis smiled. "Now go on and sit back down."

Kevin returned to his spot next to Abrams.

"Why don't you let Serena go and end all this,

Travis?" Abrams pleaded. "You wanted their attention. You got it. They'll listen now. You don't have to do this."

"But I'm afraid I do, Ms. Abrams," Travis said sadly as he deftly exchanged the scalpel in his hand for a virus laden syringe.

"No, wait," Gonzalez insisted as he limped forward. "Why don't you inject me or Abrams instead? The girl's innocent."

"No one's innocent!" Travis yelled causing Serena to scream again. "Besides, I'm doing her a favor. Who'd want to grow up under the shadow of an evil man like Brooks? Now, enough talk. You're just stalling for time, hoping the cavalry heard the shots and will arrive soon."

"No!" Abrams screamed as Travis plunged the syringe into Serena's neck vein and injected the serum.

Serena flailed her arms about, let out a piercing shriek and then slumped over. Kevin jumped from his seat and tried to go to his sister but Abrams held him back.

"You bastard!" yelled Gonzalez.

"Yes, and then some," Travis replied, "but no worse than what's been done to me."

Travis removed the syringe from Serena's neck and allowed the now semi-conscious girl in his arms to slide to the floor. He put the now empty syringe back into his uniform's pocket.

"Time to go and if you even think of doing anything stupid, I'll make you regret it," Travis said, pointing the gun at Kevin for emphasis. He then moved to and with one last glance, through the double doors exit.

He had his escape route already planned. There was another sewer access past the former infirmary rooms at the end of the corridor. Travis knew it'd only be a matter of moments before Abrams and Gonzalez would have someone hot on his trail and the rest of the building locked down.

As Travis passed one of the rooms to his right, he caught a glimpse of someone in it. He came to an abrupt halt and did a double take. He couldn't believe his eyes.

Stepping to the small glass window, Travis peered in, smiled and waved.

Wes hadn't been absolutely sure that he'd heard shots earlier but now as he looked at the face peering in at him, he was certain of it.

He'd thought of e-mailing someone but had held off. He didn't think Brooks would've been so stupid as to keep his daughter here at the Annex. But it turned out he was.

Before Wes could react to Travis' face at his door, he was gone.

Wes finally found his feet, jumped up and pressed the buzzer furiously. He kicked and pounded on the door. He even managed to crack the glass window, but the door itself wouldn't budge. In frustration, he slammed his fist against the door one last time.

After letting out an explosive breath, Wes went back to the bed and picked up his laptop. He flipped it open and fired off an e-mail to Yumiko.

He rubbed his hands and said, "Come on, come on," to himself as he waited.

It only took a moment for the response to his e-mail to come back, but it felt like forever. The reply read: The user you are trying to contact is currently unavailable. Please try again later.

Wes couldn't believe his eyes. He had to restrain his impulse to pick up the laptop and slam it against the wall. He took a breath and after a moment of thought, he realized what had happened. Yumiko was already conducting her mission at the Cage family farm. They didn't want any messages coming through that might disrupt what they were doing.

To Martin, Wes fired off an e-mail apprising him of the situation as he saw it and to notify Yumiko as well. Obviously, Travis wasn't currently at the farm if he was down here in the basement.

Wes sighed heavily as he put his hands to his head. Before he'd heard the shots, Wes had been reviewing the file Martin had e-mailed to him. It contained the information on Walter Kobayashi; the Pentagon's special investigator. It turned out that Walter had disappeared right around the time that Travis had faked his own death. Travis it seemed was as good as his word.

"I have a bad feeling about all this. I hope she gets the message before it's too late," Wes said to the empty room.

The sport utility vehicle they'd been in rested a few meters away in the clearing. At this distance of about a football field, shielded by the trees, and at this angle, no one in the farmhouse or its barn could see Yumiko and her team. But using their high-powered visual equipment, they could see everything.

"Thermal imaging is reading heat signature in the basement of the main house," the camouflaged tactical agent called out. "And it's moving."

Yumiko glanced down at her own camouflaged outfit. She'd been on plenty of raids previously. She'd done meth lab, gambling and prostitution busts. Those had gone off without a hitch but something about this one was making the hair on the back of her neck stand up.

"Ma'am?" the tac agent called out.

Yumiko shook herself to get rid of the willies and said, "How large is that signature? Is it a person?"

"Confirming..." the agent called out as he fiddled with his equipment. Finally, he said, "Unknown, ma'am. Cannot confirm. Repeat, cannot confirm. There's too much interference from some powerful electronic equipment down there."

Yumiko raised her scope to her eyes and looked through the trees to the fence bordered main house. The windows were all shuttered and the weeds in the lawn were knee high, but the path to the front door was still clear. Then, she trained her scope on the barn. It was also shuttered and run down. They'd checked with the electric and water companies, and the sewage utility. All were still in service and being paid on a yearly basis. Someone was down there using that farm for something.

The tactical agent moved away from his scanning equipment and joined his two other partners near the SUV in a final check before the breach. Brooks' team on the other side of the barn, were probably doing the exact same thing. Hell, knowing Brooks, they were probably already in the barn.

With a glance at her watch, Yumiko saw that there were fifteen minutes to go.

"We're ready, ma'am," the lead tac officer called out.

Yumiko gave him the thumbs up in return and they slowly headed toward the main house.

They crouched low, moved slowly and hid behind the trees where they could. After about 200 meters, when the trees thinned out completely, they dropped to the ground and crawled on their bellies among the bushes and weeds until they reached the low wooden fence.

As they lay there, checking for any movement in the main house, Yumiko's walkie-talkie began vibrating. They were supposed to be radio silent but Yumiko assumed it was Brooks, so she put on her head microphone and answered with a whisper, "Brooks?"

"Negative, Yumiko, this is Martin," came the voice over her headset.

"How did you get on this line, Martin? We're supposed to be radio silent. We're five minutes to zero. I'm signing off..."

"Wait!" Martin protested. "Travis got Serena. That's why I had to hack your line. He was just here."

"At the Annex?" Yumiko asked not believing it.

"Yes, and there's more, here's Wes," Martin said as he could be heard handing off the phone.

"You've got to stop the incursion," Wes said.

Yumiko glanced at the watch. Three minutes to go time.

"Impossible, Wes," Yumiko countered.

"Walter's dead. Now that Travis got Serena, all he has left is Brooks. Remember, he said Brooks would be last. Something about that farm isn't right. It's too easy. Call it off."

"Even if Travis isn't in there, the cure might be," Yumiko insisted. She glanced at her watch. A minute and a half.

"Call it off," Wes pleaded.

"I'm signing off," Yumiko said and then turned off her headset.

She watched the seconds count down on her watch.

With a minute to go, she flipped on her headset and punched in the code for Brooks' radio.

"Damn it, Yumiko! What do you want? We're a go in thirty seconds," Brooks hissed upon answering.

"We have to call it off. Travis got to Serena. There's something wrong."

"What? At the FBI building? I don't believe it. We're radio silent. How'd you get this information?" Brooks asked skeptically.

"Wes got Martin to break into our communication line..."

"Wes!" Brooks said with a scoff. "We're going in, Yamazaki."

The line went dead.

The lead tactical officer looked to Yumiko with a question in his eye as he switched his weapon from safe to live.

A second later, Yumiko could see Brooks' team emerge from in and around the barn. They quickly made it to the back of the main house.

Yumiko's eyes shifted from her tactical officer to Brooks' team and back as the seconds slipped by.

Yumiko and the tactical officer saw Brooks' team penetrate through the back door and enter the farm's main house.

"This is crazy, ma'am. If something goes wrong..." the tac officer said.

After another second or two of hesitation, Yumiko said, "Okay, let's go."

They quickly vaulted the short fence and began a crouched sprint toward the front door. Ten meters from the front door, the farm house erupted into a fireball. Yumiko and her team were blown all the way back to the fence from the force of the blast.

As debris from the explosion rained down on her, although partially stunned, Yumiko rolled to avoid the larger, more dangerous objects.

The lead tactical officer was unconscious. He'd been closer to the house when the blast hit. Yumiko crawled to him and with the help of the medical tac agent, pulled him farther back out of the way.

Once clear, they began CPR on him. He was resilient and within moments had regained partial consciousness.

Now that the lead officer was okay, Yumiko flipped on her headset communications and radioed for help. The ringing in her ears made it difficult for her to hear, but she was able to piece together that help was on the way. A medical helicopter was being dispatched immediately from headquarters and would arrive within moments.

Yumiko's hearing was getting clearer, but the medical agent still had to practically yell as he asked, "What was that, ma'am?"

"A trap. A booby-trap, actually. He laid out the cheese and we bit like a bunch of amateurs."

Wes looked past Gonzalez' bed, out of the hospital's window and onto the setting sun. Dark clouds had gathered. It looked like another storm was coming.

"Well, I guess he pulled it off. His masterpiece is complete. He's sipping margaritas in Brazil. And we're left standing around holding the bag, looking like a bunch of assholes," Gonzalez said from his propped up position on his pillows.

Yumiko rubbed the bandage on her forehead where a splinter of wood had scraped her head during the explosion. She said, "We did our job, we've got nothing to be ashamed of. We just underestimated him. He'd been planning this for years. He had us at a disadvantage. Also, our own people were hindering our efforts."

"That's the truth, the *unbelievable* truth. But still the truth," Abrams added. "Speaking of people hindering our efforts, I thought FBI security had you locked up, Wes. How'd you get out?"

"Well once Brooks' part in all this came to light, they let me go. Better to have me out and still trying to help. Which brings me back to something you just said, Matt," Wes said.

Matt pointed at himself and jostled his slung arm. He winced at the sudden stab of pain and dropped his hand, "Me?"

"Yes, you and everyone else seem to think he's gone but I don't think so. He's infected all the girls, but they're not dead, yet. Without the parents with their tear-stained cheeks on the nightly news begging the international community for help, is his revenge complete?"

They all thought about that.

Yumiko nodded and said, "If it was my daughter, I'd wait. I'd wait for the horror to really set in and for them to beg me for the cure. I'd wave it under their noses and then smash it right in front of their eyes. I'd laugh at their tears."

"So would I if I were in his place. So would we all," Wes said. "No, it's not over. He's still out there and we've still got a chance."

"Okay, I'll give you that, Wes, but Frank Alfaro and Senator Cole will never be permitted to get on TV. How do we catch him?" Matt asked.

"The one lead we had turned out to be a booby-trap. And this guy's so good at disguises, we couldn't recognize him when he was standing right in front of us," Abrams said exasperatedly. "He's a goddamn ghost."

"True," Yumiko said suddenly smiling, "but he does have one weakness."

"Which is?" Matt asked.

"To be understood," Yumiko replied. "I got a peek at the initial interview they did with the real Mr. Underwood. One of the things Underwood said, besides Cage is batshit crazy, is that Cage wanted to be understood. Someone, anyone to understand what he was doing and the implications of it.

"It's like you told me before Wes, people think they're all different but really, we all do the same things. It's just a variation on a theme."

Wes snapped his fingers and said, "You're right. The whole time, he's been leaving us little clues. Not consciously, mind you, but subconsciously because like so many of us, he still needs that validation. It's been staring me in the face but I just couldn't see it until now."

"Well, what is it?" Yumiko asked.

"I don't want to say right now. I don't want to get anybody's hopes up or have anything else happen like at the farmhouse," Wes said with caution in his voice.

"Wes..." Yumiko said.

Wes backed toward the door to Matt's room. He said, "I've got to check on something. I'll keep you posted and I won't do anything stupid if I find what I think I may find."

"Wait, Wes," Yumiko said, "at least let me get an agent to go with you. After what happened to Brooks..."

"I'll be okay. I'll call you later," Wes said as he opened and went out the door.

"Goddamn it," Yumiko said as she tried to rise from her chair. A wave of nausea washed over her and she fell back into the seat.

"Come on, boss," Abrams said. "You know the doc told you, you have to stay overnight for observation. You have a concussion."

Yumiko nodded. "You're right. You're right. So you better go after him."

Abrams took a step and winced. Her leg injury was only a flesh wound but it still stung. She turned back. "But what about you guys?"

"Well be fine," Matt said grinning. "I guess you're the boss, now."

"Follow him but keep your distance. If he gets into any trouble bail him out if you can or call the home team and we'll come running."

Abrams nodded. "Yes, ma'am. I'm on it." And a moment later, Abrams was gone.

Yumiko and Gonzalez looked at each other and shook their heads.

———

Wes paced the deserted, dusty road swinging the light from his flashlight back and forth. The road lights were few and far between in and around the national park. He wasn't actually looking for anything in particular, though. He was getting a feel for the why. Why did Travis pick this particular spot to fake his death? What was the subconscious clue that Travis had left them?

He shined his light up at the cliff above and scratched his head.

He'd already requested that what remained of the body in Travis' coffin be exhumed for DNA testing. But with the mortal blow to the FBI, Wes wasn't sure if, when or how long that was going to take. He already knew who had been in the car when it went off the cliff, though. It had been Walter Kobayashi, Travis' former torturer.

The motive for that was clear enough. Travis had said Walter would be the first and he was. It was also convenient in allowing Travis to fake his own death. For all Wes knew, the Pentagon probably knew it was Walter and not Travis in that casket, but what could they do? Certainly, they couldn't and didn't go public with that little tidbit.

No, the thing that was bugging Wes was: why here?

Wes shut off his light and stepped back up against the embankment next to his rental car. He took a deep breath and let his mind go into that dark place that was so scary to him but so powerful.

In his mind's eye he could see it. It was very late at night. A car would pass by maybe once in an hour up on that cliff road. Travis had somehow managed to capture Walter. Weeks prior to subduing Walter, Travis had already swapped his medical information with Walter's. He belted a drugged Walter into the seat. He put a firebomb in the backseat, put the car into neutral and pushed it over the edge. Wes imagined Travis watching with some satisfaction as the car burst into flames on the very road he was standing on now. Travis hadn't made the firebomb strong enough to completely destroy Walter's body but the fire was enough to obscure any of Walter's identifying marks.

The movie in Wes' mind played on. He could see Travis hidden in the dark among the trees. He even waits and watches as the police, fire truck and ambulance arrive on the scene. He laughs at them. He laughs a dark, cold laugh at them. And then he...

The movie-like images suddenly went dark but it was there. It was on the edge of his consciousness. It was like an itch that he couldn't scratch. The image was coming into focus again for Wes just as he heard the honk of a car's horn.

Wes had been so deep in his mental trance that he hadn't noticed the Toyota pick-up truck pull up alongside his rental car. The side of the truck had the emblem of the National Parks, specifically the Great Falls National Park.

A park ranger climbed out of the truck and shined his halogen light in Wes' face. Wes squinted and put up a hand to shield his eyes from the glare. The ranger said, "It's a bit late to be out on this road, sir. Is everything all right?"

Wes realized that that the ranger was Travis immediately even though Travis had tried to disguise his voice. Wes tightened his grip on his flashlight and rushed the impostor ranger intending to club Travis over the head, but stopped short when the fifty-thousand electrical volts slammed into his chest.

Travis caught the unconscious Wes as he fell to the ground.

"You're pretty quick. You almost got me, Mr. Washington. Thanks for reminding me not to be so cocky. I guess I went to the well once too often with my disguise. I should've tased you without warning," Travis whispered to Wes.

After lifting him up, Travis put Wes into the truck's cab. Then, he climbed in after him, shut the door and drove away.

Thursday — December 9

Wes could hear someone typing at a computer keyboard. There was light above him and off to the left, but Wes kept his eyes shut. He tested out moving his arms and legs but realized they were taped firmly to a sturdy, heavy wooden chair.

Thinking he'd take a quick chance, Wes cracked one eyelid and peeked. Travis was standing there a couple meters away typing away. In front of Travis appeared to be a homemade containment area. He guessed that's where Travis produced the serum. Travis suddenly turned in Wes' direction and Wes shut his eye, just in time.

He could hear Travis moving about in the lab before returning to his typing.

Wes cracked an eyelid again and looked about for anything that he could use; clues to an escape, the cure, clues to Travis, clues to anything.

There were test tubes, centrifuges, scalpels and syringes; possible weapons Wes calculated.

Classical music was playing softly in the background. That sounds like music to work to, Wes thought. What could he be working on now?

Again there was a quick movement by Cage in Wes' direction so Wes shut his eye.

Wes waited but Travis didn't move. Travis said, "Come on, Wes. You can't fool me. I know you're awake."

Not going for the gambit, Wes remained still and shallowed out his breathing even more.

Travis sighed and said, "I've got you hooked up to a remote pulse monitor that's patched into my screen. Asleep, your heart rate was running sixty-five beats per minute. About five minutes ago, it increased to about ninety."

Wes raised his head and smiled. "What no gag?"

Travis clapped his hands and laughed. "Trust me, no one could hear you."

"Okay, I give," Wes said. "You beat us all. You pulled it off and drove your point home. Everyone will know about Project Quicksand and the hell you went through at the government's hands. Now why don't you just give us the cure so we can save those girls?"

"I'm glad you've come to your senses," Travis said as he came over to Wes and tore the pulse sensor from Wes' chest. "But I can't give you the cure quite, yet."

Wes winced at the temporary pain and asked, "And why is that?"

Travis tossed the sensor in a trash basket and said, "You know, I really have to thank you, Mr. Washington. Without you, none of this could have been possible."

"Now wait a minute," Wes protested. "I had nothing to do with what happened to your daughter or you. I stopped these mad wartime experiments and I succeeded, at least for a while. What they did to those soldiers and you, was wrong."

Travis laughed his cold laugh, "You really don't know do you? I'm being literal here, Wes. Do you know how we came up with the idea of using a genetic marker to target our enemies?"

Wes shook his head. Deep down he feared the answer.

"That's right," Travis said, nodding. "Before the victim is infected, the cells are put into a state of suspended animation."

"No..." Wes whispered.

Travis continued, "A state of suspended animation based on your super soldier serum. Didn't it occur to you that the same process that allows the cells to heal could be used to harm?"

Wes could only shake his head in disbelief.

"They shared the results of your research with all the other units, especially mine. The whole time you were on television railing against what they'd done to the soldiers, they were still doing it! They were still experimenting, doing things you can't dream of. All of this is just as much your fault as it was mine!" Travis shouted.

"Okay, then kill me, too!" Wes shouted back. "Is that what you want? Do you want me to beg? Do you want me to take the blame? Why am I here? What do you want from me?"

"Your help," Travis said gazing into Wes' eyes directly.

Wes had no idea what Travis was on about so he waited. Travis continued, "Remember when I told you that I didn't know what was going to happen to you when I injected you with the serum?"

Wes nodded.

"Well, that wasn't exactly true. When the pentagon assassins injected my daughter with the non-specific marker, she developed severe osteoporosis and her red blood cell count went through the roof. Between fractures and blood clots, she didn't have a chance. The same thing will happen to you and eventually, to me."

Wes looked up at Travis sharply.

Travis nodded and said, "That's right. Somewhere along the way, I was infected also. Probably from cross-contamination from working unprotected. I realized what was happening to me when I experienced the first symptoms. Since then I've been able to use calcium supplements and blood thinners to keep myself alive until I developed a cure. I succeeded in developing a cure, but not in time. My DNA has been altered irreversibly.

"So you see, it wasn't even the government, really. Time is my greatest enemy. It has always been, I suppose. Anyway, enough of the history lesson. I need you to help me with one last project."

"Let me guess, I help you and you give me and the girls the cure."

"You're a quick one" Travis said pointing at Wes.

Wes pretended to consider the offer for a while. Lacing his voice with resignation, he asked, "What would I have to do?"

Travis smiled darkly and then moved to one of his computers. He adjusted the monitor's screen so Wes could see it.

"When I was forced into going back to work for the pentagon, I spent some of that time transferring DNA samples from some of the world's leaders from the Pentagon's database into my own."

Travis noted the look of surprise that crossed Wes' face. He said, "You didn't know about that, did you? I can see it in your expression. Well, believe it. They've got contingencies for every war scenario imaginable. I thought at the time, I could use that information to somehow help my daughter or myself. Cole and Brooks however showed me that duty to country would always trump reason and compassion so I abandoned that idea. But I'm glad I kept those samples anyway."

"My god no," Wes said. "You're going to kill the world's leaders with your serum."

Travis shook his finger at Wes and said, "Now, now, you can't tell me that the world wouldn't be better off without those fools. This could be a new start for everyone. A golden age. You and I could wipe the slate clean for the next generation, Wes. You can't deny that these rich, out-of-touch politicians have screwed things up almost beyond all repair. And that they'll keep doing it if someone doesn't stop them. We'll be doing the world a favor."

"No," Wes said shaking his head furiously. "I won't help you commit murder."

"But you already have!" Travis insisted pounding his fist on the table.

"No, that was different. There was no way for me to know what they'd do with my work," Wes protested.

"The girls will die. You'll die!" Travis shouted.

"I don't care. I won't, no, *I can't* help you," Wes said struggling against his bonds.

Travis picked up a beaker and threw it against the wall, smashing it to bits. "I thought you understood, Wes. But it's okay, if I can't convince you, maybe your friend can persuade you."

Then, Travis stormed out of the lab.

Although craning his neck as far as he could, Wes wasn't able to see what Travis was doing. He could hear him though, moving something heavy. Wes hadn't liked when Travis mentioned his "friend".

A few seconds later, Wes realized with horror what Travis had meant.

Being pushed into the lab, bound in a similar chair and in a similar fashion as he was, was Yumiko.

With strength that must've rivaled Hercules, Wes fought against the tape binding him to the chair. He even heard the tape begin to tear from his exertion but at the same time, he felt sharp pain in his arms' muscles. He slumped back into his chair as Travis parked Yumiko within arms reach of Wes.

Whereas Wes had not been gagged, Yumiko had been.

He could see from her eyes and her muffled words that she was saying his name, asking if he was okay.

"I'm okay, Yumiko. But I could ask you the same. I don't understand. How...?"

Travis said, "Agent Abrams was shadowing you. She put two and two together a bit quicker than you, Wes and contacted Agent Yamazaki while you were still up on the road. I listened in on her cell-phone call as she described finding my base of operations. I incapacitated her when she was done. Abrams is now tied up in my truck. I returned and incapacitated you. When Yamazaki finally arrived, I ambushed her as well. You've all kept me quite busy."

"You sent Abrams after me?" Wes asked Yumiko who shrugged in response.

"I told you I just had a hunch, that I wasn't sure," Wes said shaking his head.

"Enough games, Wes," Travis said as he pulled Yumiko's Glock pistol from the back of his waistband and pointed it at Yumiko's head. "What's it going to be, yes or no?"

A fraction of a second ticked by before Wes said, "Okay, you win. Yes, I'll help you."

Travis held his weapon on Wes as he cut Wes

free.

Wes massaged his bruised wrists and ankles before standing upright. Travis had returned the Glock to the small of his back and Wes glanced at it.

Travis noted the glance and said, "You can try for it if you like but I wouldn't if I were you."

"What do you need me to do?" Wes offered as an answer.

"Begin running the sequences to assemble the new viruses. Triple-check for any replication errors. I don't want anything to go wrong," Travis declared.

"And what'll you be doing?"

"I'm running computer simulations for a new delivery system. The particulate aerosols worked well on the twins but I had to get very close. I don't think that's going to work on world leaders. I'm going to see if I can't make them semi-aqueous without destroying the inherent power of the virus itself," Travis said animatedly.

Wes imagined that it felt good to Travis to be able to describe the workings of what he was doing to someone who could understand it all. He said, "So, you're talking about a liquid. You're going to make them drink it?"

"You see?" Travis asked rhetorically. "You see, you *do* understand even though you protest. The world will be a better place. Just wait."

As Yumiko watched them, she thought how right Travis was. They were actually working well together. They were becoming a seamless team as time flowed by. For one brief moment, early on in the investigation, she had suspected Wes. She had dismissed it as the evidence against Travis mounted. Now looking at him, she wondered if the shoe had been on the other foot, would Wes not have become a monster like Travis?

An hour or so had passed before Wes decided it was time to make his move. He'd bought Yumiko and himself some time pretending to go along with Travis' plan but he knew he couldn't wait forever.

He reached into the gloves fitted to the containment unit to grab the test sample he had created. Per Travis' instructions, he was supposed to check it for purity. The computer guided machine whipped the sample around in order for Wes to reach it and cap it.

Wes picked the sample test tube up and was about to cap it when he dropped it on purpose. The test tube hit the bottom of the containment unit, cracked and spilled the contents. Wes yelled and jumped back in feigned surprise.

"You fool!" Travis yelled as he hit the button for the containment unit's evaporation system. "If the sample contaminates the containment unit, we'll have to stop production and clean it. Then we'll have to start from scratch. Hours and hours will be lost. Time, you fool! Don't you understand we don't have time?"

We stepped back from Travis' tirade and pretended to slip and then fall on Yumiko. As he was falling he managed to knock over some of the notes scattered about the table.

"Enough!" Travis ordered.

Wes could feel the muzzle of Yumiko's Glock pressed to the back of his head.

"No more fooling around, Wes. Don't make me put a bullet into your friend's kneecap to show you how serious I am," Travis said coldly.

Wes put his hands up and said, "Okay, okay. No more stalling. I just--I just had to try."

Travis sighed as he holstered the gun in his pants waistband. "What would you give to have

Chiang-Mei back?"

Wes turned on Travis with his fists raised. "How dare you talk about my wife?"

"Answer the question."

Wes hesitated before dropping his hands. "Anything."

"Even murder?" Travis teased.

After a long pause, Wes repeated, "Anything."

"And if you couldn't get her back but another option presented itself?" Travis asked rhetorically.

Wes nodded and returned to the containment unit.

Travis said, "Don't think for a moment that I loved my little girl any less than you loved your wife."

Wes considered that in silence and then said, "Looks like you evaporated the sample in time. No contamination. I'll have another sample up in minutes."

"Proceed," Travis agreed with a nod of his head.

As the work continued, Wes hoped that his ruse had gone undetected. He thought it had but Travis played dangerous games. He might wait for Yumiko to make her move just to have an excuse to kill her.

Travis had taped Yumiko's hands palm down on the chair's arms. With the scalpel Wes had surreptitiously slipped her, Yumiko was slowly and methodically cutting the tape that was restraining her right hand.

Travis had his back to her so when her right hand was free, Yumiko took the chance and cut the rest of her bonds. She cut the tape on her left wrist and left leg quickly enough but when she began cutting the tape holding her right leg, Travis noticed her movement out of the corner of his eye.

"Hey, don't" he shouted as he simultaneously

reached for his weapon.

Wes tackled Travis and wrapped his arms around him as Yumiko cut the last of her bonds and stood up. She swayed from the sudden rush of blood from her head but managed to stay upright.

Holding Travis was impossible. The strength he exhibited was supernatural and after a few seconds, he was able to throw Wes off. Wes was sent crashing into the opposite wall which he bounced off of and fell to the ground.

But those few seconds Wes gained were all Yumiko needed in order to get close enough to plunge the scalpel into Travis' neck.

A shot rang out as Travis managed to pull the trigger once before dropping the Glock. But Travis hadn't been able to raise the weapon high enough and the bullet went harmlessly into the floor.

Travis clutched the scalpel but wisely did not pull it out. If he had, he would have died instantly. He tried to say something as his eyes rolled widely in his head but only blood-choked croaks came from his mouth.

He stumbled to the main computer he had been working on as Yumiko scooped up her weapon and trained it on him. Travis looked back at her and seemed to smile. He punched a sequence of keys on the keyboard before falling to the ground apparently dead.

Yumiko stepped to Travis' corpse and with a finger on his neck vein, verified that he was indeed gone. "Okay, yeah, he's dead. How are you, Wes? Are you hurt?"

"No, I'm okay. Thanks to you," Wes said with a sigh of relief as he eased up from the floor.

"He was insane. We had no choice," Yumiko said regrettably. Wes nodded a silent agreement.

"Now do you think we can find what we need in these files somewhere?" Yumiko said returning to their mission.

"I don't know if you heard us in here, but he told me the secret basis of his work; my Super Soldier serum. I admit it was a shock to me, but now that we know, even if he managed to wipe his files, we could probably figure out the cure anyway. Let's hope it's still in here though," Wes said as he stepped to Travis' central computer.

"Uh oh," Wes said with a look of alarm as he stared at the screen.

"What's the problem?" Yumiko asked as she stepped closer and peered at the screen over Wes' shoulder.

In the center of the screen was a digital clock readout, counting down. It currently read: 04:30. Underneath that was a flashing cursor.

"Shit! It's a booby-trap. Just like the one back at the farm house. We've got to get out of here. Now!" Yumiko said as she stepped back toward the exit.

"I don't think we'll make it. We don't even know where we are. But there's a field here for a password. I think I can figure it out," Wes said as he broke out into a sweat.

"We're in an old, abandoned maintenance room of the park. We came through the tunnel and sewer system in the hills of the Great Falls. I wasn't completely unconscious after Travis ambushed me. I heard the water splashing and could see the tunnels when he brought me down here. I can get us out of here. Now come on," Yumiko ordered.

Wes glanced at the clock. It now read: 03:50. "Are you positive you can find the way out? What if we take a wrong turn and end up back in path of the explosion?"

Yumiko hesitated, "No, I'm not positive, but are you? Are you sure you can figure out that password?"

Wes turned to the screen and typed in: Isabella.

The computer beeped, flashed the words, 'Access Denied' and then returned to the countdown which now read: 03:05.

"How about Quicksand?" Yumiko offered. "That was the project name. Or hourglass? The present he sent to Wilhelm."

Wes typed in 'hourglass'. The beep sounded, 'Access Denied' flashed and the countdown resumed; 02:45.

Wes took a big cleansing breath, shut his eyes and went into the dark recesses of his mind. He focused on the images, sights, and sounds of Travis Cage. He saw Travis' daughter Isabella. He imagined his wife Carmen. He saw all the people from Frank Alfaro on down who'd wronged him. Although he tried to remain focused on Travis' life, somehow images of Chiang-Mei kept appearing. He couldn't understand why he'd be thinking of her at this crucial moment. What was his mind trying to tell him?

Wes' eyes flew open like window shutters. He typed in the word and hit enter as the seconds on the readout slipped from ten to nine. The readout changed from nine to eight. Had he been wrong? No, finally, the readout stopped completely and the screen switched to the desktop, revealing all of the files.

Yumiko let out a huge breath and clapped Wes on the shoulder. "I wasn't sure if the bomb or having a heart attack would get me first."

"Sorry about that, Yumiko," Wes said. "But thanks for hanging in there with me."

"What was the passcode anyway?" Yumiko asked now that they were safe.

"Time," Wes said. "I don't know why it took me so long to figure it out. Travis has been beating me over the head with his message but I didn't get it till just now. We'd all give anything for just a little more time with the ones we love. That's what the hourglass really meant."

Yumiko nodded. "You miss her don't you?"

Wes didn't have to ask who the 'her' was that Yumiko was referring to. He said, "More than you can imagine."

"He took my cell. Doubt it would work down here anyway, but we've gotta get a message out. Abrams is still out there somewhere. She might be hurt," Yumiko said as she searched Travis' body for the phone.

"Anything?" Wes asked.

Yumiko shook her head.

Wes checked the computer and found that Travis had patched into an email server. Quickly, he fired off an email to Martin back at FBI headquarters.

As they waited to be rescued, they scoured the rest of the computer files looking for the cure.

———

Wes was leaning up against Yumiko's sedan when he saw her come out of the Annex's front double-doors. She waved briefly and he returned it.

When she was near enough to hear, he said, "So how did your debriefing go?"

Yumiko laughed, then. Wes thought it was the most beautiful thing he'd heard in a while.

"They told me to take a vacation. A nice long

one. And when I get back, there'll be a promotion waiting for me."

"Congratulations," Wes said.

"I hate it had to happen this way, but..." Yumiko said letting her words trail off.

"Yeah, Brooks was a monstrous asshole but I don't know if he deserved to die," Wes offered. "Did you get the update on the girls?"

"Yeah, Martin told me that they're all doing fine. Thanks to you."

Wes shook his head. "Thanks to us. I wouldn't be here right now if not for you."

"And speaking of that," Yumiko said as she punched Wes' arm—hard. "You didn't tell me that you'd been infected, too, Wesley Washington."

"Sorry, but I didn't want to worry or distract anyone from the job we had to do," Wes grinned.

"Well," Yumiko said as she punctuated her words with playful punches. "If you ever lie to me again, you *will* be dead 'cause I'll kill you myself."

Wes stopped smiling as he warded off the blows. He said, "Yumiko, we both know we've gotten close these last few days but I don't know if..."

Yumiko put a finger to his lips. Wes stopped speaking and she said, "When you're ready. No rush, Wes. I'll be here, when you're ready." Then, after removing her finger, she kissed him quickly.

Wes held Yumiko's gaze as he thought about Chiang-Mei. He was sure she wouldn't mind. In fact, she'd probably be happy for him. He could just hear his friends and family telling him that he'd grieved enough, but still he wasn't sure. Then, he heard a voice in his head that actually convinced him.

As Yumiko watched Wes' face, she was surprised and glad to see him finally smile a genuinely happy smile.

He said, "So where are we going on this vacation of yours?"

Yumiko laughed and clapped her hands together. "Ever been to Cancun in December?"

"No, and it sounds fantastic."

"What changed your mind?" Yumiko asked as she took Wes' hand in her own.

"Travis," Wes replied. "I could hear him in my head asking me if I'd learned nothing from all this."

"And have you?" Yumiko asked as she looked into Wes' dark brown eyes.

Wes paused before speaking. Finally, he said, "Time's not your enemy. It's your friend. It's always there to remind you to enjoy your life while you can. And that's exactly what I'm gonna do; enjoy every damn minute of it."

Epilogue

Secret U.S. Government Program Revealed
Senator Cole loses bid to become president under
scandal
By Rick North, Independent Press

A secret government program dubbed, Quicksand, has been revealed. It was a program designed to infect and subsequently kill United States' enemies at home and abroad who fell into the category of terrorist. This program came to light from the heroic efforts of one, Travis Cage; a now deceased, former military intelligence scientist who blew the whistle on the deadly and illegal biological weapon program.

Senator Cole, through her involvement in this unauthorized program has abandoned her presidential election bid and given up her seat as the Chair of the Senate Intelligence Oversight Committee. She has also announced that she will be retiring from public service completely at the end of her current term.

There has been much speculation that her daughter's death was somehow linked to the illegal Quicksand program. Other former high-level officials have been linked to the scandal as well, but have not responded to requests for information. Also, Wesley Washington, who was involved in the former Super Soldier hearings, has been reportedly linked to this scandal as well. This has not been confirmed as Mr. Washington is out of the country and unavailable for comment.

The international community has been in an uproar for the past few days and is expected to lodge complaints with the United Nations for sanctions against the United States for possible war crimes...